DIAMONDS ARE FOREVER

BY:
BROOKE ST. JAMES

Diamonds Are Forever

Published in Nashville, Tennessee, by Elm Hill, an imprint of Thomas Nelson. Elm Hill and Thomas Nelson are registered trademarks of HarperCollins Christian Publishing, Inc.

Elm Hill titles may be purchased in bulk for educational, business, fund-raising, or sales promotional use. For information, please e-mail SpecialMarkets@ThomasNelson.com.

ISBN 978-1-40033-3011

Other titles available from Brooke St. James:

Another Shot:
(A Modern-Day Ruth and Boaz Story)

When Lightning Strikes

Something of a Storm (All in Good Time #1)
Someone Someday (All in Good Time #2)

Finally My Forever (Meant for Me #1)
Finally My Heart's Desire (Meant for Me #2)
Finally My Happy Ending (Meant for Me #3)

Shot by Cupid's Arrow

Dreams of Us

Meet Me in Myrtle Beach (Hunt Family #1)
Kiss Me in Carolina (Hunt Family #2)
California's Calling (Hunt Family #3)
Back to the Beach (Hunt Family #4)
It's About Time (Hunt Family #5)

Loved Bayou (Martin Family #1)
Dear California (Martin Family #2)
My One Regret (Martin Family #3)
Broken and Beautiful (Martin Family #4)
Back to the Bayou (Martin Family #5)

Almost Christmas

JFK to Dublin (Shower & Shelter Artist Collective #1)
Not Your Average Joe (Shower & Shelter Artist Collective #2)
So Much for Boundaries (Shower & Shelter Artist Collective #3)
Suddenly Starstruck (Shower & Shelter Artist Collective #4)
Love Stung (Shower & Shelter Artist Collective #5)
My American Angel (Shower & Shelter Artist Collective #6)

Easy Does It (Bank Street Stories #1)
The Trouble with Crushes (Bank Street Stories #2)
A King for Christmas (Novella) (A Bank Street Christmas)
Diamonds Are Forever (Bank Street Stories #3)
Secret Rooms and Stolen Kisses (Bank Street Stories #4)
Feels Like Home (Bank Street Stories #5)
Just Like Romeo and Juliet (Bank Street Stories #6)
See You in Seattle (Bank Street Stories #7)
The Sweetest Thing (Bank Street Stories #8)
Back to Bank Street (Bank Street Stories #9)

Split Decision (How to Tame a Heartbreaker #1)
B-Side (How to Tame a Heartbreaker #2)

Cole for Christmas

Somewhere in Seattle (Alexander Family #1)

CHAPTER 1

Galveston Island, Texas
June 1988

*I*t was one of those days where the weather was perfect. There were just enough clouds in the sky that the sun would occasionally go behind them. But even when the sun was out, the temperature was so wonderful that it felt like the air was made of nothing.

I sat on the end of the dock, letting the gentle wind hit my face. The sun went behind a cloud, and the breeze was so pleasant that I smiled even though no one but God was there to see me.

Mac was with me, but he was lying down with his eyes closed. It was a Saturday afternoon, and the two of us were on an adventure. The nap was a planned part of it. Mac was outgrowing naps, but when he took them, he preferred doing it outside. So, on days when I wasn't working at my family's hardware store, we tried to plan our excursions around letting him sleep outside for a little while.

It worked out for me because it gave me a few moments of quiet time. Mac's naps had gotten significantly shorter during the last year or so, but I still managed to get some thinking and writing done during them.

I was just about to finish another Garden City notebook. It was a collection of stories for kids about a town of woodland creatures that existed in a community garden. Theoretically, there were humans around, but they didn't behave like humans in the real world. The humans in Garden City weren't curious about woodland creatures. The children didn't chase or try to play with them. Everyone just sort of ignored the animals the same as they would a flower or tree. I thought maybe one day I'd write about a little human child who got curious and came into their world. But for now, the two didn't intersect.

As far as the forest creatures went, there were lots of side characters in the stories, but most of the action was centered around a family of hedgehogs. Hank and Barbara were the parents, and the children were Timmy, Tommy, and Tess. Tess was my aunt's name, but I couldn't think of a name I liked better for the character, and Aunt Tess was happy to have a hedgehog daughter named after her.

I had been working on the Garden City series for so long that I had enough material to write twenty children's books. I knew they might not ever get published, but I was definitely going to try for that after I put together a more polished series.

The problem was that I was missing illustrations. I had tried, but I had no talent for drawing. I had thought about making them chapter books just to get around the little obstacle of pictures, but I always imagined my stories with pictures to complement them, so I felt like I'd be settling if I got impatient and tried to reformat them into chapter books. I thought I should wait until I got some illustrations squared away to search for a publisher.

My Aunt Tess was a successful painter, so she had the skills to help me out, but she had teenage kids of her own and a busy life, and I didn't feel right about asking her to sign onto my project, which, as of now, was a hobby. She knew I was writing the stories, and I told myself that she'd offer if she was interested.

At this point, I was content to write as much as I could and try to deal with finding a publisher and illustrator later. I was fully aware that, as a single mother with a toddler, I should probably get my head out of the clouds and stop writing about woodland creatures. But my parents had always been extremely supportive, and they didn't seem like they were in a big hurry for us to move out and be fully independent.

Mac and I had our own little place on their property. It was a detached apartment—a little mother-in-law cottage in my parents' backyard. My dad had built it as a shop when I was in middle school. He used it until I got pregnant, at which point, they decided to remodel and turn it into an apartment so that Mac and I could have our own place. One might wonder how a young lady such as myself ended up being a single mother at such a young age.

Let's just say a lot of stuff had gone down during my junior year of high school.

The short of it was that I fell madly in love with Bradley Clark.

He was the star quarterback and the most popular boy at my school (and probably even all of Galveston). We dated for all of my sophomore and part of my junior year.

At first, it was amazing. I had always been the quiet girl, and I was easily charmed by Bradley who knew and had the respect of everybody in our town. I actually thought he loved me, and I got swept away by my own feelings.

All I can say is that the choices I made seemed justifiable at the time.

I had been with Bradley for long enough that I thought it would last forever. I ended up pregnant, and that was the end of our relationship. Bradley didn't take it well when I told him. He got mad and accused me of cheating. And then, knowing that wasn't the truth, he resorted to crying like a baby and begging me to take matters into my own hands and put an end to it. I told him I would think about it, but I knew I couldn't do it. I went back to him the next day to tell him that I was going to have the baby.

During that conversation, he basically told me it was my responsibility since he already voiced his opinion about it. He was out. He washed his hands of us without a second thought. He asked me to lie and say that he wasn't the father because he had a big life planned with a football scholarship, and this unplanned pregnancy would ruin everything for him.

We broke up, but I didn't tell anyone I was expecting a baby at first. I knew if I said I was pregnant but that it wasn't Bradley's I would come off looking like a tramp who had cheated on her boyfriend.

I stayed quiet during the first four months of the pregnancy, and when I say I stayed quiet, I mean I barely spoke at all. I had gone through a lot in my early childhood, and I had a few other episodes when I got 'quiet', but none were as long or intense as the one when I was first carrying Mac.

Everyone assumed it was because of the breakup with Bradley. My parents finally figured it out after a few months, and they came to me saying they knew—that they could tell.

I broke down and told them everything, and they decided to help me keep the secret.

We didn't do this as a favor to Bradley. We did it primarily because we didn't want Bradley to have the right to be in the baby's life after he made it clear that he didn't want to be. We stayed quiet about it until I couldn't hide it any longer, at which point, I got pulled out of high school and continued school at home.

I was sure a few of our close family knew the truth about Bradley being Mac's father, but even now, almost four years later, no one ever talked about it. I was just the girl who got pregnant in high school and was now a single mom. It was entirely possible that people talked about it behind my back, but no one had ever even asked me who Mac's father was. Maybe they all just assumed it was Bradley and didn't say it.

Either way, Bradley now played football at Baylor and was extremely successful like he thought he'd be. He had never met Mac, who was now three-and-a-half years old.

Mac had been my partner since the day he was born. I loved that boy with all my heart, and there was never a time, even in the midst of sickness or sleepless nights, when I regretted keeping him. He was my masculine protector from day one. By the time he was one, he was catching lizards and hunting snakes. At two, he was protecting me from other various forms of scary wildlife like spiders and stinging fish. He was hilarious and passionate, and we were as close as any mother and son had ever been.

Thankfully, my parents helped us afford a comfortable lifestyle, considering my circumstances. They were content to let Mac and me live in the detached apartment. They owned a hardware store, and I worked there thirty hours a week. My mom usually watched Mac when I was working, but Dad was happy to babysit, too, and so were my brothers, both of whom lived at home.

I showed up at the hardware store, did tasks, and helped customers. I did that because I needed to make money for Mac and myself. But I was never so happy as when I was in my own head, visiting my characters and exploring their fictional world. I had no lack of inspiration. In fact, it was as if the stories had already happened and I was just in charge of recounting them.

At the moment, I was thinking of a scene that took place in Badger's Bakery while Mac was sleeping soundly next to me. My eyes were closed but I knew he was there because my hand was on his motionless leg.

I drew in a deep breath, relishing this perfect day and imagining I was Barbara Hedgehog, heading into Badger's bakery to pick up my order of teacakes (which would later be spilled because of an incident with Tommy coming into the bakery on his skateboard). I pictured the scene and smiled at the sight of teacakes flying through the air like graduation caps.

We were on the bay side of Galveston, so the water was calm, and our surroundings were green with tall grass and cattails at the shore. We were at the state park on a quiet, hardly used dock that extended into a small bay called Oak Bayou.

Mac and I spent a lot of time near water when we were outdoors for our adventures. There was always something for him to do near water—some bug or fish to catch, or sea creature to find.

I was sitting there, imagining Garden City and searching for the set-up before Barbara headed into the bakery. I was seeing the scene in my mind's eye when I heard the sound of a boat's engine.

I opened my eyes as the engine sound grew closer. It looked like a man was in the boat. I glanced around, but Mac and I were the only people in sight on the shoreline.

I sat for a moment, looking at the water, watching the boat as it approached. Mac stirred and sat up as it came closer. I figured it wouldn't make it all the way to the dock because of how shallow the water was, but it kept getting closer and closer.

"Huh, who's that?" Mac asked, instantly sitting up, looking preciously protective.

"It's just a boat," I said. I was calm and assumed the best, but I had two brothers and a father with a military background, so I was always prepared for a fight. I wasn't expecting trouble, but I did have a good-sized knife in my bag, and I wasn't scared to use it if I had to.

The boat's engine stopped, but the guy waved at us like he might come over.

"It's too shallow!" I said, yelling at him and waving him off, urging him not to come to us. But he kept coming. It was a large boat and he killed the engine and began using a pole to push himself into the shallows.

I stared at the guy, trying to see if he was someone we recognized. He appeared to have some facial hair—not much but a little. I couldn't tell how old he was. Young, it seemed. I had been so focused on Mac for so long, that I forgot what eligible men my age looked like. I smiled at myself for thinking this guy was eligible. He was handsome, I could see that in spite of the ballcap and the sunglasses.

"What's he doin'?" Mac asked skeptically, standing up as he eyeballed our visitor.

Mac had a fake coonskin cap and a bow and arrow set with suction cups. He put on his hat and stood proudly by my side, puffing out his chest. I was sitting on the dock so we were about the same height. I smiled at Mac's intense expression as he watched the man push his boat through the water. It was low tide and shallow where we were but his boat came closer and closer.

He was someone I did not recognize, but he was extremely handsome.

It wasn't like me to go around noticing men. Considering the fact that I ended up a pregnant teen, I was fairly innocent with men. It wasn't like I went around checking-out guys and trying to date them. I hadn't even been that way when I first got with Bradley. He was the one who had approached me. With him, I had honestly thought I met the guy I'd spend the rest of my life with. I wasn't trying to be promiscuous. In fact, it had taken him a year to convince me that it was okay.

I went into that relationship with an embarrassing amount of naivety. I thought I had found the one. I imagined Bradley and me pairing up, staying together forever, like geese.

All this to say, it was a bit odd for me to notice a man's looks—especially since I had Mac. But this guy in the boat was handsome enough that I couldn't help but notice it.

CHAPTER 2

Andrew Klein III (Drew)
Son of Senator Andrew Klein

*D*rew left the Galveston Country Club in a bad mood. He wasn't sure where he was going, but he had to get out of there.

His dad's flats boat was the nearest form of transportation. He got on it and took it into West Bay, cruising and letting the wind hit his face.

It wasn't his dad's fastest boat, but it got the job done. It took him away from everyone else.

Just moments ago, Drew's life had changed.

He found out some news about his girlfriend, and his future took an unexpected turn, one of an infuriating nature. And seeing as how he was spitting mad, it was lucky that all he did was leave abruptly. Drew had nearly started throwing punches at his best friend, Sam.

Drew showed Sam the engagement ring he had just bought for Jocelyn, at which point Sam broke down and told Drew that Jocelyn had cheated on him. Drew didn't believe it at first, so Sam admitted that he was the person she had cheated with. Sam said he knew he would lose Drew as a best friend, but it was worth it to him to save him from marrying her, since apparently, she had been the one to approach Sam.

Drew didn't know what to believe. He knew it had happened, but other than that, his head was swimming. He was positive it had happened because Sam gave details about the time and place, and some specifics about Jocelyn that he wouldn't know if things hadn't happened between them.

Drew closed his eyes at the sick feeling that washed over him as he remembered the things Sam said. He steered the boat straight ahead into the open waters.

Maybe he would do something reckless and spiteful to make himself feel better. He had the ring with him. He had just shown it to Sam, and he shoved it back into his pocket during the conversation. Drew slowed a bit, but he continued to steer the boat as he took the ring out of his pocket.

It was a five-thousand-dollar diamond ring and he nonchalantly tossed it overboard to let it sink into West Bay, never to be found again.

He was satisfied with himself for doing that.

It was therapeutic to let it go and not care where it landed.

Only it didn't go far enough, and it landed in the boat. It somehow, miraculously, didn't make it out of the boat. Drew saw it drop out of the air and heard it clang as it hit the floorboard.

Drew blinked in disbelief. He was an athlete. He played baseball and football growing up. He had an awareness of how far things would travel based on their weight. Not only that, but the boat was traveling fast enough that the ring should have gone over.

He tossed the ring overboard.

He knew it should have gone over.

But it was still there, in the corner of his boat. He blinked at it, wondering if he was seeing things. He slowed down and stopped the boat just long enough to step away from the helm and pick up the ring.

Sure enough, the ring was there in the corner of the boat. Drew stared at it. He wondered if it was possible that his muscle memory had failed him. He figured it could've been his fault for not aiming properly or throwing hard enough, but it all felt weirder than that.

He wondered what would happen if he tossed it into the water now that the boat was still. It crossed his mind that there might actually be an imaginary force field that would just hold the ring in the boat.

He was about to give it a shot. He reared back with every intention of throwing the ring overboard again. But just before he let it go, he caught sight of someone sitting on a dock in the distance. It looked to be a woman.

He knew what he had to do the instant he saw her. It was one of those times in life where he knew what his next move was without even thinking about it. Drew would give this ring to a stranger instead of wasting it at the bottom of West Bay.

She was a long way off, but Drew started that way, traveling fast as he entered the lagoon where she was sitting at the end of the dock.

He smiled when he noticed a young child. It seemed like the boy was lying down at first, but he stood up next to the female. Drew couldn't get a read on her facial expression, but either way, he was sure she wouldn't mind being handed a valuable piece of jewelry.

The whole point of the flats boat was that it could traverse shallow waters. Drew needed that feature at this moment. There was no way he could get up to this dock in a regular boat. He cut the engine and started using a pole to push himself closer to the dock.

The young boy stood tall, bowing up to Drew as he approached. He had on a Davy Crockett hat and was aiming a suction cup arrow right at Drew. The woman tried to warn Drew of how shallow it was, but Drew knew his boat would be fine. He lifted a hand from his pole, palm out in a gesture of surrender to the boy, who was staring at him intensely.

"I come in peace!" he yelled.

"What's your business here at Blackberry Bay?" the lady asked.

"Is that where I am?" Drew asked, looking around as he continued to push the boat closer. He could tell she was making that up, and he wondered what kind of woman would do something like that. He was intrigued instantly. "I have something that I wanted to give to you."

"Whatcha got?" the young boy said, nudging his chin at Drew in such a confident way that Drew had to laugh.

"It's a piece of jewelry," Drew said.

"We didn't lose any jewelry," the girl said.

"I know, but I still wanted to give it to you," Drew replied.

He could not tell how old this woman was. She was small-framed. He wasn't sure if she was the boy's mother or his big sister. The boy stepped in front of her, but she held onto him. He thought he was doing the protecting, but she was being protective. She had on sunglasses and her long dark hair blew in the breeze. She was a lovely young woman, and Drew felt relieved that the ring didn't sink to the bottom of the bay.

"What's your name?" Drew asked.

The boy started to say something, but the woman, pulled him back, stopping him. He looked at her, and she whispered to him. She then held her shoulders straight and introduced them. "I'm Lady Lollipop, and this is Prince Lionheart."

"Who's he?" the boy said, smiling and pointing to Drew but looking at the lady.

"He's a pirate," she said widening her eyes.

"I am?" Drew asked.

"A real pirate?" the boy asked at the same time.

He was adorable. He had big brown eyes and one of those kid accents where he mispronounced some words. He was serious, staring at the lady with his eyebrows furrowed.

"Yes," she said with a wink. "A real pirate. He's Captain Jack."

Drew wondered how she got away with both confirming he was a real pirate and winking at the same time.

"Naw," the boy said, looking at the lady with a sideways smile like she was trying to pull one over on him. "He doesn't even have an eye patch."

"Not all pirates have an eye patch," Drew offered.

"Are you a pirate?" the boy asked, looking at him.

"He is," the lady said, answering for Drew even though Drew would have told him that he wasn't. The boy looked at her, and she gave him a little wink, letting him know she was still playing pretend.

"Okay, maybe I'm a pirate, but my name's not Captain Jack," Drew said.

"What is your name?" the boy asked.

"It's Captain Drew."

"Captain Drew?" The boy said, cocking his head to the side. He squinted, inspecting Drew closely. "Are you nice?"

"I think I am," Drew said with a groan, giving the boat one last push. "I try to be." He was only a few feet away from the end of the dock by then, so he stopped using the pole and stashed it on the boat.

He smiled at the two of them as he walked the few feet to the other side of the boat. They were quite a pair. They were matching somewhat with dark pants and white shirts. The woman had long hair and a delicate, beautiful smile, but her clothing was boyish. She wore an oversized white button-down shirt with brown, loose-fitting high-waters. Her clothes were definitely cleaner than the boy's, though. He was something else. And that hat was just too much. Drew had been in a terrible mood, but he couldn't help but smile at the boy.

"I have something to give you," Drew said.

He held the ring in his hand, leaning over the edge of the boat, reaching for the woman. She was a little reluctant, but she stood up, got to the edge of the dock, and reached out for it.

"What is this?" she said, looking at it.

"It's a ring," Drew answered, even though that was obvious.

"I was wondering why you were handing it to me." She tried to hand the ring back to Drew, but he took a step back and put his hands up, insisting that she keep it.

"Wait, I can't take this," she said.

"Why not?" he asked.

"Because it's not mine."

"It is now. I'm giving it to you."

"Yeah, he's giving it to you," said Prince Lionheart.

17

"But it belongs to someone else," she said, still holding it out even though Drew had backed away and was too far from her to reach it.

"I can assure you it doesn't belong to anyone," Drew said.

"See? He said you could have it," the boy said.

"How do we know it's not stolen treasure?" she asked, looking at the boy.

"He said he was nice, Mama, he didn't steal it."

"Did you?" she asked, turning to look straight at Drew as if it was a serious question.

"No. Why would I... I bought it."

"Is it plastic?"

"I promise you it's not plastic," he said, shaking his head and wishing it was.

"This is big," she said, staring at it.

"I know."

"So, why are you handing it to me?" Her expression was confused, wary. She was gorgeous without a stitch of makeup. It registered to Drew that the boy had referred to her as his mother, but he didn't think much of it. She looked young, but she could be old enough to have a child, he supposed.

Drew shrugged at her question. "Because my other option was to throw it in to the water. I almost did that. I tried to. But then I saw you, and I thought it was better for me to give it to you than to toss it overboard and let it sink."

"Yeah, but why are you getting rid of it?"

"Because I intended to give it to a woman, and now I'm not giving it to her. I'd rather just not see it anymore."

"Well, Captain Drew, I really do appreciate the kind offer of letting me keep someone else's priceless jewelry, but I couldn't possibly."

"Toss it then," Drew said nonchalantly.

"What?"

"Toss it. Just throw it in the water if you don't want it."

"I'll throw it!" the boy said, stepping up to the challenge, holding his hand out.

The woman clutched the ring in her fist and drew it away from the boy. "Just a minute," she said.

Drew shrugged. "You'd be better off selling it at a pawn shop than tossing it into the water, but it's up to you."

"Why don't you just give it to the person it was intended for?" she asked.

"That's out of the question."

"What if you change your mind?" she continued insistently.

He gave her a sardonic smile. "I won't." He moved to grab the pole again so that he could push the boat into deeper waters and lower the engine.

He loved meeting these two. They were both adorable. He had been in a dreadful mood. He still was, but they had taken the edge off. He smiled inwardly thinking he'd always secretly wanted to be a pirate.

"Wait," she said.

Drew hesitated, waiting to hear what she'd say.

"This is crazy."

He shrugged. "Not any crazier than meeting Prince Lionheart and Lady Gumdrop."

"Lady Lollipop," she said, absentmindedly glancing at the ring and then up at him.

"Keep it," he said. "Pawn it if you want. Use the money for something else. You're doing me a favor by taking it off my hands."

"Uh, I, I, I don't know what to say."

"You could tell me your real names."

"Mac and Lucy," she said, stiffly.

"I'm Mac," the boy clarified, making Drew smile. "We came out here on the dock, and right when my mama was telling me the story about the hedgehogs and Garden City, I fell asleep and took a nap because Pap taught me how to sleep outside under the stars because the stars are still up there even though you can't see them in the day."

The boy was speaking quickly, and Drew didn't quite get all of it, so he looked at the boy's mother for help with translation.

"He said he was taking a nap outside, like his Pap taught him."

"He said something about a hedgehog, too." Drew looked at the boy. "Are you out here hunting hedgehogs with your bow and arrow?"

"Naw, you don't hunt hedgehogs," Mac said. "There's not even any wild ones around here. They go in cages. We have pet hedgehogs at our house. They live in their cages. I never even hunt hedgehogs. I just pet 'em and hold 'em on my lap. They won't poke you if you hold them real still." He shook his head, staring at Drew seriously. "You're not supposed to hunt hedgehogs—only snakes and rats and spiders and roaches."

He was passionate, speaking with enthusiasm. It was adorable, and the sheer cuteness distracted Drew and prevented him from understanding all of the words. This boy was tough as nails and preciously passionate in his speech and mannerisms.

"Did you say you have pet hedgehogs?" Drew asked looking at the boy.

"Yeah!"

"Yes sir," the mother corrected.

"Yes sir. My mama got two pet hedgehogs so she could learn how to draw them, but she couldn't do it right, so now they're just our regular pets. But we can't let Sport catch 'em because he's a huntin' dog, and he'll eat 'em."

"My parents have a Dachshund named Sport," Lucy explained when Drew looked at her.

"There was the part about Sport," Drew said. "But there was also something else. Why'd you get hedgehogs? To do *what* with them?"

"So she could learn how to draw them," Mac said.

Drew still couldn't quite understand. "To do what?"

"Draw," Mac said. "Like a picture."

"Oh, *draw* them." Drew regarded the woman curiously. "You wanted to *draw* a hedgehog?" he asked, still not understanding.

"It's a long story," she said shaking her head.

And Drew stared at her, feeling like he was in the mood to hear it.

CHAPTER 3

———— ⌾⌾⌾ ————

Lucy

*T*his man on the boat was full of surprises.

He was a complete and total stranger. I had lived in Galveston all my life, and my family knew a lot of people, and I still had no idea who this guy was. He showed up on a boat, pushed himself over to us with a pole like a Vietnamese fisherman, and handed me a diamond ring.

It was pretty much the last thing I expected would happen when he came our way. He had been wearing a neutral expression when he approached, and my initial feeling was to be concerned, like maybe he was out looking for a lost person or even a dog. He could have asked for directions from here to London and it would have been less weird than what actually happened. He could have invited us on a tour of the bay in his boat and it would be less shocking than handing me a giant, seemingly real, diamond ring. He also seemed undaunted by the fact that I introduced myself as a made-up character and told Mac that he was a pirate.

He was about to push out into deeper waters and leave, but then he brought up hedgehogs. I told him it would take a while to explain the fact that I was a hopeful children's book author. And then I thought twice about it and realized maybe I could just come out and say that.

"I'm trying to be a children's book author," I said. "I guess I am one by now. I've written a lot of books. I have a little series about a hedgehog family, and I thought maybe I could illustrate them myself if I had some real hedgehogs. But they're really hard to draw. It turns out I'm a way better storyteller than I am an artist."

"And now you're stuck with two pet hedgehogs?"

"I wouldn't say I'm *stuck* with them. They're pretty cool pets."

"Do you study them for inspiration?" he asked. "You know, watch them and see how they interact with each other for your books?"

I let out a humorless laugh. "They actually don't interact with each other at all. I didn't know that about them when I got them, but they're not social. They want to be in separate enclosures. We get them out and socialize them with us, but we do it separately. I wondered if it would be a mistake to represent a hedgehog family in my books when they aren't social in real life, but then I remembered that the ones in my story also walk on their hind legs and wear clothing, so I figured it was okay."

Mac cracked up when I said that. He had heard me say that exact thing to someone else. He knew the timing of my joke, and he was waiting for me to say it so that he could laugh on cue.

"The hedgehogs in your book wear clothes?" Drew asked. (I assumed his name was Drew since he had said 'Captain Drew' earlier.)

"Yeah, I mean, I don't really talk about it, but yeah, they do have clothes. When I imagine how they live, it's with clothes on. I'll have the illustrator draw them that way. Kind of like Beatrix Potter's animals."

"Or Looney Tunes or DuckTales," he said. "Lots of cartoon animals have clothes.

"Bugs and Daffy don't have clothes." I said, thinking of Looney Tunes.

"No, but Elmer and Porky do. And... Yosemite Sam."

I smiled. "Yosemite Sam's a man," I said.

Mac laughed even though he wasn't quite following us. He had gotten distracted by the boat which was drifting closer to the dock again.

"What's the book about?" Drew asked.

"What? Hedgehogs."

"No, you already said that. I meant what do the hedgehogs do?"

"Oh, all sorts of stuff. There are other animals, too. The badger has a bakery. It's a town with all sorts of little creatures. It's just that the hedgehogs are the main characters."

"Do they have names?" he asked.

"Of course. Timmy and Tommy and Tess."

"Timmy, Tommy, and who?"

"Tess," I repeated. "Those are the kids. Mac likes them because they have all sorts of adventures and get into a little trouble." I winked at Mac who reared back dramatically as if passing out.

"And Tommy shot a bow and arrow in a contest one time, and shewwww—" Mac made a dramatic noise as he picked up his bow, squinted, and pretended to shoot an arrow off the dock.

Drew laughed at Mac. It was a good-natured chuckle like he was laughing with him and not at him.

"I would really like to read this book," Drew said.

"My mom has forty and twenty books full of it," Mac said. "You can read the one where the frog's tongue got stuck on the ice, and he was like ooh, ooh, ooh…" Mac wiggled around, indicating what a bind the frog had been in.

"There was a scene in one of them where a frog got his tongue stuck to the fencepost," I explained.

But we were distracted. Mac was getting to the edge of the dock, closer to the boat, reaching out.

"Can he come onto the boat?" Drew asked, coming to our side again.

"Sure!" Mac said.

"Wait, baby, I don't know," I said.

"You could come too," Drew offered easily. "If no one's looking for you right now. I can take you guys on a quick boat ride."

"I don't know."

"I've had an odd afternoon, and I could use the distraction."

"I guess you have had an odd afternoon if this wound up in my hand," I said, raising the fist that was holding onto the ring.

"Yeah," he agreed, nodding at me. "Odd is an understatement. Talking to you and little Mac about hedgehogs seems like the best thing I could possibly do with my life right now."

I laughed and moved toward the boat. "All right, but we can't go far," I said.

"Yessss," Mac said, getting to the very edge of the dock excitedly. He made little jumping motions as Drew came to the side to help him onto the boat.

"Don't jump off or anything," Drew said to Mac after he set him down on the boat.

"I won't, don't worry," Mac assured him.

"He won't," I said. "He goes on boats all the time."

Drew turned as I was saying that and reached out to help me on. I didn't need assistance, but I was already headed that way, going toward Mac, when Drew turned and reached out to catch me. He put one hand on my waist and the other on my arm, steadying me.

I tried not to flinch, but I stiffened slightly because my body reacted to him. He was handsome and he smelled nice, and I felt that same dangerous, gut-tingling attraction I had from way back with Bradley.

"Oh, I d-didn't need any help, okay, thanks. Thank you." I reached out to try to give him back his ring.

"No, no, no," he said. "If I take it from you, I'll just toss overboard. I'm not kidding. Please take it. Sell it. Save it. Give it away. I don't care."

I put the ring in my pocket because I could tell how serious he was about me keeping it. My pants were loose-fitting, and I made sure the ring was situated at the very bottom of my pocket so it didn't fall out.

Once I was settled onboard, Drew smiled at me and nudged his chin toward Mac. "Little man is so cool."

I smiled. "I wasn't lying when I said he was Prince Lionheart," I said.

"I see that."

We were smiling at each other as I made my way to the seat to sit next to Mac. "So, does that make you Princess Lollipop?"

"Lady," I said.

"Princess Lady?" he asked, misunderstanding on purpose.

"Lady Lollipop," I answered, smiling at him.

"Lollipop, huh? Why did you pick that?"

I shrugged, thinking about that. "I do like lollipops," I said. "Candy in general. There's a cool candy store in Garden City. It belongs to the turtle. I love the looks of candy. It's bright and cheerful."

"Okay, so, Lady Lollipop and Prince Lionheart. Welcome to my boat. What sorts of adventures did you two get into today?"

He spoke in his best imitation of a tour guide, using the pole to push us into deeper water.

"Can I help you?" I asked, starting to stand again when I saw that he had to push harder with the extra weight in the boat. "No, no, I've got it, sit down with the young prince and tell me what you did today."

"My mom went to work in the morning, and I stayed at Nana and Pap's, and then Mom came back, and we ate chicken nuggets and tater tots and then, after we went on our walk, I took a nap on the dock and then your boat motor woke me up and we took a boat ride with you."

Drew listened closely, trying to hear everything Mac said. "What'd you see on your walk?" Drew asked.

"Mac hunts and keeps the path clear of snakes and snapping turtles," I said.

"Good man," Drew said.

Mac nodded with a totally serious expression.

Drew used the pole to guide us into the open water in the middle of Oak Bayou. It was a small area that was open only on one side like a longer version of a lagoon, and he pushed us into the middle of it. He put the engine down and started it, taking us slowly into the bay.

Mac and I rode in boats all the time with my father, uncle, and grandfather. I was happy that Drew handled the boat carefully just like any of them would have.

We rode a little way into Dana Cove before Drew found a place to stop. I thought he was going to turn around and head back right away, but he didn't. He killed the engine and let down the anchor. He had a fishing pole stashed in the back of the boat and he grabbed it.

"Would you like to cast the line a few times, Little Mac?"

I liked that Drew called him Little Mac. He had other people in his life who called him that, and I always liked it. Little Mac was a video game character that had gotten popular just before Mac was born. I hadn't named him Mac for that reason, but it worked out that way because my uncle Billy was a famous boxer, and Mac spent a significant amount of time in his boxing gym. Uncle Billy was retired now, but he still coached and he owned the gym on Bank Street.

People called Mac *Little Mac* all the time in reference to that boxing video game character. Uncle Billy said all the time that he hoped Mac would grow up to follow in his footsteps. I was adopted, and Billy was in the family by marriage, therefore he and Mac weren't even close to blood-related, but you couldn't tell. Billy loved having Mac at the gym. No one ever spoke of me and my brother being adopted by Daniel and Abby King, so Mac knew nothing of it. I was sure he'd hear something one day, but for now, it didn't seem relevant.

"Little Mac is a character on a boxing game," Drew said, talking to Mac.

"I know, and I can box like him, too. I go train at Bank Street all the time when my mama's at work. It's right across from Pap's store, and you can catch me over there just about… what Mama? Three times every week? I even take my own class. And I go there when Evan and Jacob and Will are in there boxing, too."

Drew glanced at me, trying to keep up. "He practices boxing at the gym with his cousins and his uncle," I clarified.

Drew nodded. He cast the line and handed the pole to Mac who was standing on the bench seat next to me. I had a hold of him, and he fished all the time. He knew what he was doing.

"Are you from Galveston?" I asked Drew. It would seem like I would know him if he was.

"Houston," he said. "My parents have a camp over here, and we come play golf. Today, I was here with a friend of mine. He's the one who told me about the… he told me… anyway, that's why I'm getting rid of that ring, because of something he told me. I took off after we talked, and that's when I saw you guys. He's still waiting for me. He rode here with me. It's going to be really weird on the way back to Houston. I might even make him get another ride. I don't know. Maybe he did me a favor. I'm sure he did." Drew was speaking casually, laughing it off, but I was sure it was more of a heartbreak than he was making it out to be. I knew it had something to do with the ring, and I assumed there was a woman and a breakup. I looked at Drew who was looking out at the line.

31

"Reel it in a little," he said to Mac. "And watch that cork in case you get a bite."

"Don't worry, I am," Mac said.

"Just say 'yes sir,'" I said.

"Yes sir," Mac said. He glanced at Drew to make sure Drew wasn't upset about his lapse in manners.

"You're doing good," Drew said. "Although we might not trick any fish with that fake worm."

"Maybe you can come fishing with me and Pap sometime. He knows where to get you some shrimp."

"I'd love that," Drew said.

"Listen, if you want to go on my Pap's boat right now, we can just go over there. He'll take us on it anytime we ask him to, and it's *a lot* bigger than this."

"My dad's at work," I said, shaking my head apologetically. "There's no way Pap could go fishing right now. And his boat's not much bigger than this one."

"Yes ma'am, it is. It's way bigger," Mac said, glancing behind him at the boat and being brutally honest without meaning to hurt Drew's feelings.

Mac glanced at me after that, and I leveled him with the motherly stare that said I didn't want him to say any more about it.

"It's okay," Drew said. "This is my baby boat, anyway."

"What other boats you got?" Mac asked.

"We have several. A speed boat, a party boat, a sail boat."

"I rode on a sailboat one time," Mac said. "With Pap."

"Is Pap his dad?" Drew asked, looking at me.

"No, no, it's my dad," I said. I made a tiny shift in my expression—there was a small regretful edge to my smile as I looked at Drew. He got the idea that I didn't want to mention Mac's dad. I could tell he understood by the way he looked at me.

"I got one, I got one," Mac said, hunching down and growing rigid. Drew instantly came to stand behind him, holding onto him, even though I had a grasp on him as well. I let go once Drew got fully behind him. Drew helped him reel it in, but the fish got away.

"Aw man, that was a big one, too!" Mac said.

"Do you want to do it again?"

Mac nodded and Drew cast the line again.

CHAPTER 4

"Then we went fishing until *all day* because it took us so long to catch one, and even when we did, it was just an old catfish, so we cut it loose, and then we went back to the dock, and it was almost dark outside, so Mister Drew said he would walk us back to our car since he couldn't see it from the dock and he didn't want us to go back by ourselves."

I could hear Mac spilling his guts from the other room, and I cringed, knowing it sounded like more than it was. I went into my parents' living room to meet Mac and my dad. We planned on eating dinner with my parents and we had come back later than expected, so my dad was already a little worried when we came in.

"What is he talking about?" my dad asked, staring at me with a confused, concerned stare.

My father, Daniel King, recipient of the Congressional Medal of Honor. He was a military man and a very protective father. It had taken a lot of restraint for him to keep from confronting Bradley when all that happened with Mac. It had eaten my dad up to stand by and watch Bradley not do the right thing, and he had been on high alert with me and men ever since.

"What's he talking about going out fishing and walking you back to your car in the dark? Mom said you and Mac just went walking."

"We did at first, but Mac laid down to rest and then we met a nice guy who took us on a boat. Mom's taking leftovers out of the fridge," I added. I bent down to pick up Mac and I began going back toward the kitchen with him on my hip.

Dad was curious about this new information and he followed us like I knew he would. "Where were you?" he asked.

"At the park—at that old dock over on Oak Bayou."

"What happened?" Mom asked, hearing our conversation as we went into the kitchen.

"Where are Phillip and Evan?" I asked, thinking of my brothers. I wasn't trying to cut her off. I was already asking the question before she asked hers.

"They ate and took off," Mom said, answering me.

"I thought y'all were just going for a walk," Dad said.

"What happened?" Mom asked, confused. "What'd they do?"

Sport was running around and getting excited during all of this, adding to the chaos.

"We went fishing all day with Mister Drew," Mac answered.

"It wasn't all day," I said. "Just a few hours."

"But all we caught was an old catfish, so we just cut it loose. Mister Drew had a pocket knife on him."

"You went fishing?" Mom asked, looking at me.

"Yes."

"With someone named Drew," Dad said. "Who carries a knife, apparently."

They were hilarious. I could see why they were concerned about me with men after what happened in high school, but goodness, it had been almost four years since then.

"And Mister Drew gave mama a diamond ring, and she said 'no' to him, and he said he was going to throw it off the boat, right into the water if she didn't keep it."

In true Mac fashion, he made a throwing motion and said the whole statement with passion and excitement.

Mom and Dad both looked at me.

They knew how much of a storyteller I was, so I could tell they weren't sure if Mac was reciting true events or not.

I took a deep breath. "We did meet a guy named Drew, and he did give me a diamond ring, but it's not as crazy as it sounds."

"Did he propose marriage to you?" Dad asked. His expression was so confused that I couldn't help but smile.

"What's propose marriage? "Mac asked.

"He didn't propose anything," I said calmly, answering them both. "I get the feeling that he's super loaded because he was just about to throw that ring out of the boat like it was nothing."

"What's super loaded?" Mac asked.

"It means he has lots of money. Let momma tell the story. I only got bits and pieces of what happened from Drew because I didn't want to come right out and ask him about it, but basically I think he was about to propose to a woman and his friend told him something bad about her that made him change his mind."

"So, this guy was a total stranger who came up to you and gave you a ring after he was about to give it to someone else?" Dad asked, still not quite getting it.

"It wasn't a big deal that he gave it to me. He literally said he was going to hand the ring to me or toss it into the bay."

"And I would've dove down and got it," Mac assured us all.

"So what? He just gave it to you, and you walked away, free and clear?" Dad asked.

"Well, yes. He gave it to me, and then we went fishing for a few hours. We were out there so long that someone came by looking for him."

"Who?" Mom asked.

"I don't know. One of his friends. He only stayed for a second. Drew just told him to wait for him at the marina. He liked Mac a lot. They got along really well. I felt like it was one of those God things—like Mac and I were put there at the right time and place to help him out. You know how Mac is. He can brighten anyone's day. I think this guy really needed it today. He left there a lot happier than when he came."

I thanked my mom when she set plates of food in front of Mac and me.

"And when did the diamond come into the picture?" Dad asked.

"He gave it to me first thing when he came up to us," I said. "I tried to give it back several times. Even at the end, when he seemed like he was in a good mood, he didn't want it back. He insisted I take it. He was honestly going to throw it out."

"That's weird. Do you think he'll come around wanting it back?" Mom looked at Dad as she asked the question.

"I'm never even going to see him again," I said. "He was really nice, and he meant it when he said he would toss the ring if I didn't take it."

"What's his name?" Mom asked.

"Drew."

"Captain Drew," Mac said.

"Is he a Captain?" Mom asked.

"No. He's a lawyer. Almost. He still has to take the bar exam. He said his dad's a lawyer, or used to be. I think he does something else now. He said that his dad still has a law office."

"Where? Here?" Dad asked.

"Houston," I said.

"What's his last name?"

"I have no idea."

"Captain Hook," Mac said, still stuck on that pirate thing.

"He's not like Captain Hook," I said to Mac. "He's a nice pirate. He's not a pirate at all. We were just teasing about that."

"I know," Mac said, chewing his food.

"Do you still have the ring?" Mom asked.

"Definitely." I reached into my pocket for it. "I keep checking to make sure it's there."

I set the ring on the bar where we were eating. My mom gasped and reached out for it, picking it up and bringing it right in front of her face, staring straight at it intensely from only inches away.

"This looks *real*, Daniel," she said to my dad, sounding astonished.

"It is real," Mac said in his little toddler voice, sounding confident and certain.

My dad reached out for the ring. Mom gave it to him, and he held it up to the light. "That's twice the size of your wedding ring," Dad said, sounding stupefied.

"I know," Mom said. "It's huge. What was he thinking?"

"He was done looking at it. He wanted it away from him. He wasn't kidding when he said he'd throw it in the water. I could tell he was serious."

"We need to take this to Mr. McCain," Mom said, referring to the local jeweler.

"If it's real, you shouldn't go getting too attached to it," Dad said.

"Why? He gave it to me. Can I get in trouble for having it?"

"No, but he's probably going to come to his senses and come back for it," Dad said.

"Can he do that?" Mom asked.

"He told me more than once to sell it," I said. "We don't even know how to get in touch with each other. There's no way he could find me even if he wanted to."

"How old was this guy?" My dad was still playing investigator.

"He was a man," I said. "A young man. Maybe mid-twenties. However old you are when you graduate from law school and ask someone to marry you."

"The gold is real," Dad said, inspecting the inside of the ring.

"Does that mean the stone is too? "Mom asked.

"I have no idea," Dad replied.

"Well, even the gold alone has to be worth something," Mom said, looking at me excitedly. "Maybe you can sell it and use the money to hire somebody to illustrate your books."

She knew that was what I wanted most.

"I already thought of that," I said. "Wouldn't that be amazing? I almost hate to get my hopes up, though. I keep thinking it's too good to be true."

"I keep thinking that too," Dad said as he set the ring on the counter.

Mom reached out and picked it up again. They were fascinated by it. I couldn't say that I blamed them. I was fascinated too.

***

That night, after I put Mac to bed, I wrote for a long time.

I wrote a whole adventure where Tess Hedgehog went on a walk and met a stranger, a dashing rabbit named Jack. In the story, Tess helped Jack out of a bind, and in exchange for her help, he gave her a diamond ring. She, of course, insisted that she couldn't accept it, but Jack claimed that he found it anyway and it meant nothing to him.

In the book, Tess gave the ring to the Garden City Public Library (which, at the beginning of the book, was nearly out of business due to lack of funding).

It wasn't unheard of for me to use personal details like this as inspiration for my stories. In real life, though, it was likely that I wouldn't be as heroic as Tess Hedgehog. I liked the idea of giving the ring to someone else—finding a way to do something charitable with it. But I was already attached to the other idea—the one of me hiring an illustrator. I had thought of that before my mom mentioned it.

My parents weren't jewelers, but they had thrown around the word "thousands" several times when they were looking at that ring. I felt excited at the possibility of approaching an illustrator with a budget. My parents didn't charge me rent, but I had other bills, and I worked to buy food and gas and pay my way in the world. I had a little saved, but it would have taken me a long time to save thousands.

I thought maybe this was my big ticket. I thought that maybe if I had Garden City illustrated the way I liked, it would be easier to pitch to a publisher.

I was excited about keeping the money from the ring, and I really hoped it would work out where I could.

CHAPTER 5

Two months later
King's Hardware
Bank Street

"*L*ucy King, come over here, girl!" Samantha whisper-yelled to me as soon as I walked in the door of the hardware store. "Come here and let me talk to you before you even go put your purse in the breakroom." She was glancing around shiftily as if we were on some sort of secret mission. I couldn't imagine what was so important. I had seen her only thirty minutes ago, before I left on my lunch break.

"What is it?"

"Somebody came in for you!" she said.

"Who?"

"A guy. A fine, fine, fiiiiine guy. I'm talkin' fine." She was still whispering urgently. "And your dad's not gonna tell you about it. I bet he's not because he looked all wigged-out."

"Wigged out? About what?"

"The message."

"What message?"

"Back up, back up, back up, and I'll tell you." It was busy in the store, and Samantha pulled me down an aisle so we could be alone. "He came in just after you left. He was asking for you. He talked to Belinda, but you know how she is. The first thing she did was run and tell your dad."

Samantha was so intense, that I could hardly keep up.

"Who was it?"

"He said his name was Captain Drew. *A Captain.* Can you believe it? Already a Captain at such a young age. Anyway, so he was asking if you were here, and Belinda said you had gone to lunch, and he told her to give you a message. He said to *meet him at seven o'clock tonight at the normal place!* He even said to dress nice."

Samantha was so overcome with excitement about the whole thing that she spoke slowly and her voice became about three octaves deeper with dramatic emotion. Her eyes were still huge and she wore a serious expression.

"And you better believe that Belinda went straight to your dad and told him everything."

"What'd my dad say?"

She shook her head. "He asked if the guy mentioned his last name, and Belinda said he hadn't, and then he thanked her and told her not to tell anyone what happened. But I saw his face after that, and he *did not* look happy."

"Did you hear the guy say this stuff with your own ears, or did you just hear Belinda repeat it to my dad?"

"No, I heard both. I heard the guy say it, and then I went and listened to Belinda telling your dad. I could see him when he walked in. He's seriously so fine, Lucy. Who is he? How do you know him? What's your *secret spot*? What's he talking about?"

"I have no idea," I said, shaking my head and acting confused.

She had asked me about ten questions at once, so I got away with being vague. Samantha could not keep a secret, obviously, so I wasn't going to tell her anything. I was thankful, however, that she had told me the whole thing happened.

"Thank you," I said. "Thanks for telling me that. I'll have to think about it. Did you say he said his name was Drew?"

"Yes. Captain Drew. Can you believe that? I thought he must be in the military, like your dad. Captain sounds high-up. How do you know him? I bet your dad knows him."

"No, no, I'm going to have to think about it," I said vaguely. I made a face like I was really considering it, even though there was no puzzle to solve.

I only knew one Drew.

It had been a while since I had seen him, but the memory was scorched into my mind. It wasn't every day that someone handed you a diamond ring.

I had ended up selling the ring. I held onto it for a month before I did it, but it was gone now. I made that deal with myself. I kept it for a month just in case Drew decided to hunt me down to get it back. But I sold it a while back. Mr. McCain said it was worth five thousand dollars, but he gave me thirty-five hundred dollars for it. I felt extremely lucky to receive that amount.

I hired an illustrator in Houston to do three complete books. That cost two thousand dollars. I had new tires put on my car, I bought a new stand for my television and some new shoes for both myself and Mac. And then I had saved the rest. I really hoped Drew wasn't contacting me to try to get it back.

"Did you say that guy said for me to dress nice?" I asked when the thought crossed my mind.

"Yes," Samantha said. "Why? Did you figure out who he was? Do you know what it means?"

"No, I just think that's weird that he would say that. What does nice even mean? A dress? I don't really do dresses. A skirt, maybe."

She shrugged. "Well, first you have to figure out who it is."

"Yeah, you're right," I said nodding. "Thanks Sam."

"Don't tell your dad I told you," she said.

I shook my head. "Don't worry, I won't."

I was nervous for the rest of the afternoon.

Belinda did not mention Drew's visit to me, and neither did anyone else who worked at the hardware store. My dad didn't give me the message either, but that was no surprise. If Samantha hadn't said something, I would've never gotten word about it.

All afternoon, I went back-and-forth, changing plans. First, I thought I would go meet him at the dock, but not dress up. I would take Mac with me and wear the same Huck Finn get-up that I was wearing the first time we met. Then I decided I would go without Mac and that I would get all dressed up. I changed my mind a few times before deciding what to do.

I asked my mom's friend, Evelyn, to watch Mac while I went to meet Drew. I told her I was going out fishing with a friend, mostly because I couldn't imagine what else we would be doing out there.

Mac was happy when I told him he was staying with Evelyn. He loved to go to her house because she always had ice cream. I didn't tell my parents about it—at least not for tonight. I knew Evelyn and Mac would both mention it to my parents the next time they spoke, and I wasn't going to keep it from them, but I didn't want my dad to try to prevent me from going tonight. I guess it was one of those times where I decided I wanted to ask for forgiveness rather than permission.

My parents weren't accustomed to keeping track of Mac and me. We often went over to other peoples' homes and didn't check in with my parents about it at all. Usually, they didn't even notice when I pulled into or out of the driveway. Tonight, I didn't mention where I was going.

I was wearing jeans and a button-down, cap-sleeve blouse. I tried to tell myself I didn't care what Drew thought and that jeans would have to be good enough, but I picked out a simple skirt that went with my blouse and shoes and stashed it in my purse, just in case. I styled my hair and wore a little makeup, but I certainly didn't look "dressed up" by most people's standards. There was no glitter or sequins or high heels.

Evelyn did tell me I looked too pretty to go out fishing. She said it to me using sign language so that Mac wouldn't hear. Evelyn and I spoke in code the whole time because of Mac. I knew how much Mac loved to go out on the water, and I didn't want him to catch wind that I was going there and beg to come. I told Evelyn I'd be back in a couple of hours, and she told me to take my time.

I was extremely nervous about meeting Drew. It wasn't because I was excited, thinking I had any sort of romantic possibilities with him. I was nervous because I was afraid he would ask for the ring back. It had been two months since he gave it to me. The encounter was still fresh in my mind, but I had convinced myself that he had forgotten about it. I hoped he had.

It made me feel anxious that he had sought me out and could possibly ask me for the ring back. I assumed that was what this whole thing was about. I had been thinking about it all afternoon, but I couldn't mention it to anyone else, so my thoughts had gotten away from me several times.

I reasoned that if worst came to worst, I could borrow the money from my parents and just work off what I owed them over time. But then I worried that it was more about the ring itself than the money. I hadn't even considered that it might be a family heirloom. I told myself that Mr. McCain, the jeweler, would have some information if Drew ever needed to track it down.

Needless to say, I had done a lot of thinking by the time I pulled up at the trail that led to the dock at Oak Bayou that evening. I parked on the side of the road just like I did every time I went there.

The sun was extremely low in the sky. I knew it might be dark by the time he came to the dock. If he came at all. *What was I doing?* It would be dark soon, and I hadn't planned for that.

I quickly searched the backseat of my car, knowing that Mac usually kept a few adventuring supplies back there. Sure enough, there was a plastic, battery-operated lantern. It was red, but Mac had scratched and scuffed it. I pressed the button, smiling when it came on.

It only took a few seconds to lock my car and head toward the dock. I had to walk down a short trail, but it wasn't far at all.

Drew was not in the water when I got there, and my first thought was that he wasn't coming at all. I was honestly a little relieved about that. But I was five minutes early, so I figured I would stop drawing conclusions and be patient.

I sat on the end of the dock. The water was high, and I took off my shoes and rolled up my jeans, letting my toes dangle in the water. Usually, by this time of night, Mac and I were doing other things and our outdoor adventure time was over. I stared at the place where the sunset had been, thinking we should get outside more at this time of evening.

It was a minute or two after seven when I saw Drew's boat coming toward me. It was dark enough that I wasn't a hundred percent positive that it was Drew at first, but the closer he came, the more certain I felt that it was him.

I was so ready for this encounter to be over—or at least get settled about the ring. I stood up and got myself back in order. I walked around in a circle to dry off my feet, then I adjusted my jeans and put on my shoes before picking up my bag and the lantern. It was getting darker, and I waved the little lantern where he could see it. Drew did the same maneuver where he cut the engine before pushing himself up to the dock.

He was dressed sharply in slacks and a button-down shirt with a suit jacket.

"Hey stranger!" he said, smiling and in a good mood.

I felt a wave of relief that he didn't seem to be worried about the ring.

"Hey Captain," I said, teasing him for telling Belinda that earlier.

He laughed.

"My coworker was really impressed," I said. "She thought you were an Army Captain."

"She would have still been impressed either way," he said, smiling confidently at me.

He pushed the boat near the dock and I got to the end to help him catch it from bumping the side.

"I've got it. Don't hurt yourself," he said, moving to my side of the boat. "Thank you for meeting me here," he added. "Where's little Mac?"

"With a friend."

He looked behind me as if searching for clues about my current situation. "Can I borrow you for a little while?" he asked. "For an hour or two?"

"What for?"

"A party."

"What kind of party?"

"A dinner party."

"I already ate dinner."

"You don't have to eat," he said. "You can just pretend to."

I let out the breath I'd been holding since he came up to the dock.

"What?" he asked.

"I'm just relieved. I thought you were going to ask me for the ring back."

He made a face like he had no idea what I was talking about. "I told you I don't care about that thing. I hope you got rid of it. I didn't even remember it existed."

"What's this dinner about?"

"It's for my dad. It's a bunch of people he knows. That girl I used to date got herself invited through one of my dad's friend's sons. She's going to show up tonight, and I would really like to just have…" He trailed off, making a pleading expression. "It would be helpful if you would pretend to be my girlfriend while we're there. You don't have to, but it would get her off my back."

I stared at him. "Where is this thing?"

"At Palm Beach." He gestured behind him. "It'll only take like ten minutes to get there from here. And we don't have to stay all night. I just wanted her to see that I'm with somebody else. I mean, not with, but… we don't need to do anything, she'll just assume we're together if you're there with me. I just don't want to have to talk to her. I feel like she's just there to try to get me back, and I don't want to deal with it tonight."

I shrugged. "I don't mind doing it, but the problem is I'll probably know someone there. My whole family's from here. We have friends who go to Palm Beach all the time. I know someone who works over there."

"It's not open to the public. It's at Palm Beach, but it's private. It's a party for my dad and a few of his colleagues. You probably won't know anyone there. And it really wouldn't matter if you did, honestly. You don't know her, and that's all that matters."

I nodded. "I'll do it, yeah, I'd be happy to." I glanced down at my own appearance. "I wasn't quite prepared for a fancy dinner party, though. I didn't know what to wear."

He took a second to look me over. "I really don't care. I think you look great. Please come."

"I brought a skirt to change into, but I'm not sure that it'll be any better than these."

"Are you kidding? You have a dress with you? That's perfect. Put it on."

"Not a dress. Just a skirt. But it'll go with this top." I pinched the front of my shirt. "This is the only shirt I have with me, so it'll have to do."

He smiled brightly and gave an excited clap. "Thank you so much for this."

"You're welcome," I said. I was so relieved he wasn't looking for the ring that changing into a skirt and going to a dinner party to pretend to be his girlfriend felt like a walk in the park.

"I'm going to change into the skirt," I said, as I started going back toward my car. "But you have to be honest with me about how it looks when I get back. If it's not nice enough for the party, it would only take me about twenty minutes to run home and get something else."

"I would seriously be fine with you wearing what you have on right now," he said.

"Okay then, just wait here and I'll be right back."

I had a skirt that fell above my knees, and I made quick work of getting it on. I ran back onto the dock as quickly as I could in my new outfit.

Drew was smiling at me when I came back down the dock. "Oh my gosh, thank you, you look amazing," he said. He scanned my appearance. "You look like you planned for this. Let's go."

Chapter 6

———

rew helped me onto the boat, and we set out from Oak Bayou, heading toward Palm Beach.

This beach was the biggest news in Galveston right now. It was part of a place called Moody Gardens, and it was a gorgeous, man-made, white-sand beach on the bay side of Galveston. Earlier this year, tons and tons of pristine, white sand had been shipped on barges from Florida to build this beautiful new attraction. I didn't realize how dark Galveston's sand was until that white sand arrived on our island. It was powdery and beautiful. I had been several times since it opened, but never to a private event. I had no idea what to expect.

Drew was trying to get there quickly, so we didn't talk much on the way to the party. We left his boat at a marina and took his truck from there. He had a huge, brand new Ford Bronco. I had to take two steps up to get into it.

"This is a cool truck," I said, checking out the inside once we were on our way to the party.

"Thank you," Drew said. "It was a graduation gift."

"Wow," I said, looking around. "What a gift."

I turned to look at him, taking in his profile as he drove. He was smiling. He was so good-looking that it crossed my mind to wonder why in the world he needed a fake date.

"What do these people think?" I asked. "Do they think you have a girlfriend already? Is there anything I should or shouldn't say? Maybe it's smart for me to keep quiet so I don't say anything wrong. Who's all going to be there?"

Drew had the radio playing, but he turned it down, smiling at all my questions.

"My dad's a State Senator," Drew said. "It's a party for him. It's his birthday. There's probably going to be about a hundred people—some from Houston, and some are his politician friends from other cities."

He stopped speaking, and I was quiet for long enough that he glanced at me.

"Are you okay?" he asked.

"I just got really nervous," I said, causing him to laugh a little.

"Don't be," he said. "We'll fly under the radar. I just need to be there to support my dad, and I'd rather not have to encounter certain situations."

"And you think having me stand next to you is going to solve that problem—keep this woman from coming up to you?"

"That's the plan," he said with a shrug.

"Am I supposed to make up a fake name and a whole identity?" I asked. "Do I need to be someone special?"

"You are someone special," he said, ever the gentleman.

I couldn't help but smile. "Seriously," I said.

"No," he answered, shaking his head. "Just be yourself."

My first thought was that I should definitely not mention Mac, but I didn't say that. I just knew I wouldn't mention my son to any of these people. I hoped I wouldn't get into a situation where I had to deny having children, because I obviously wouldn't do that, but I also wasn't planning on bringing it up—especially since I was supposed to be Drew's girlfriend.

"Is there a designated amount of time that you and I are supposed to have been dating?"

"A month or so," he said. "Nobody will ask us. I've come to Galveston a few times recently, so they'll assume I was seeing you. My folks will definitely go along with it. We've all been busy lately, and they don't know who I'm seeing."

"Is it okay for me to say my regular name and everything?"

"Lucy King? Yeah."

"What's your last name?" I asked. "My dad was asking me, and I had no idea."

"Your dad was asking about me?" Drew asked, glancing at me with a confident grin.

"When I brought home the ring," I said.

"What'd you do with it?" he asked.

"Why, you don't want it back, do you?"

"No."

"Good, because I sold it."

59

"To who?"

"A jeweler."

"How much?"

"Thirty-five," I said.

"Thirty-five dollars?" he asked, grinning, teasing me.

"Hundred," I corrected.

"That's pretty good," he said, nodding easily. "Better than in some fish's belly."

"I wonder if that's ever happened," I said. "Where a fish ate something valuable and someone took it home to cook it and got rich."

"That's definitely happened," he said. "Don't you think?"

"I would think so," I said. "It happened that one time in the Bible."

"Where the whale ate Jonah?" he asked.

"No, where Peter found a coin in a fish's mouth. Enough to pay a tax he owed."

"Well, see, there it is. It has happened before."

"Yeah. I guess," I said. "But that one was more like God put it there."

"Yeah, but how do you know He didn't use some little kid to do it?" Drew said. "Maybe it had been in there for two weeks, in that fish's mouth, because a kid threw it into the river."

I shrugged, thinking about it. "Maybe God used a human to get it there. I guess we'll never know. I'll add it to the list of things I'd like to ask God when I see Him."

We pulled into the parking lot at Palm Beach. I was slightly nervous about going inside, but not as much as I thought I would be. I felt an odd sort of confident calmness, like I could put aside any insecurities or reservations and enjoy the evening. I was looking forward to being someone else for a little while.

Other than going to work, I honestly didn't get to get out of the house much by myself. It wasn't that I didn't have the ability to go out and do things, I just had fun hanging out with Mac, and we had settled into a routine. I enjoyed being a mom.

"Do you really have a list, or were you joking?" he asked, drawing me from my thoughts before we got out of his truck.

"A list of what?" I asked.

"Of things you want to ask God."

"Oh, yeah, I definitely have a list."

"What else is on it?" he asked.

"Hmm, where did the dinosaurs go? Why did He make mosquitos, flies, wasps, centipedes? Goodness. Centipedes, why? I kind of wish we didn't have those. Also, why do babies get sick? Is Elvis really dead? Did my parents make it to heaven? That one will probably be obvious, but you know, stuff like that."

"Whoa," Drew said, reacting quietly but with a stunned look about my last statement. He had been smiling during most of it, but his smile faded when I mentioned my parents. "I'm sorry about your folks."

"It's fine. I was five years old. Our parents got into a car accident. Me and my little brother got adopted after that. It's been a long time, and Daniel and Abigail are mom and dad to us. We have another brother, Evan, who once punched a kid in the face for saying I was adopted." I shook my head a little, giving him a reassuring smile. "I'm fine and everything. In a way, I'm thankful it all happened. In the time after they passed and before I went to live with Mom and Dad, I had experiences that… anyway… that's part of the reason I can imagine things like I do. I learned how to do that when I was little, and I can tap into fantasyland anytime now." I smiled and shrugged.

"Wow, I guess everybody sees the world a little different," he said. "We all have such different takes on life."

"Yeah, we do, and all sorts of things factor into our perception. We were born a certain way, with natural genetic features and tendencies, and then you have to factor the way we were raised and the people we were exposed to. All sorts of combinations can happen. No two people are exactly alike. Even twins who have things lined up with their genes and upbringing still turn out different. I have cousins who are twins, and they're crazy different."

Drew stared at me. I had no idea what he was thinking. "You're… different, too," he said. He hesitated at his choice of words, cringing at himself.

I smiled since I didn't take offense to it at all. "Thanks," I said, casually reaching for the door handle.

"I did mean it as a compliment," he said, getting out of his side of the truck.

"What about you?" I asked as we began walking toward the entrance. "Tell me something about your filter."

"What filter?"

"You know, the one we were just talking about. The one you see life through."

"Oh, well, according to the song by Creedence Clearwater, I'm a *fortunate one*, whatever that means, probably that I'm a spoiled brat."

"*It ain't me, it ain't me.*" I sang out, making him smile. "*I ain't no fortunate one*," I continued, leaving out the part where they specifically say, *I ain't no senator's son.*

"Yep, exactly," he said, smiling.

"Does everyone think you're spoiled?" I asked.

He shrugged. "Probably, and I'd be lying if I said I wasn't a little spoiled, in some regards. But money doesn't equal happiness. There's a lot of stress in my dad's job, and he and my mom have issues and stuff. We've always had money, but I never really got their attention or anything. Also, I'll do it, and I'll be good at it, but it wasn't really my idea to be a lawyer. That was all my parents."

"Really?" I asked looking at him. "You're going to spend the rest of your life doing a job you don't like? That's terrible. Don't do it. Your parents won't be mad at you very long if you decide to do something else."

He let out a little chuckle. "Yes, they would, but it's okay because now that I'm this far into it, I see where I can be useful in one area of the system. I'll be a lawyer for a while and then I'll become a judge. I may change my mind once I'm doing it full-time, but I think that aspect of it could be a calling for me."

"A judge, huh? Interesting. That's cool. With the robe and gavel?"

"Yeah."

"Neat. You'll need lots of wisdom for that."

He chuckled again. "Yes, you're right, I will."

"Do judges actually decide if you're guilty or not? And tell you how long you have to go to jail?"

"In small cases, maybe. But, no, in bigger cases the sentence is established and the jury would take care of the verdict. It's more about managing the courtroom, making sure the trial is orderly and fair—that the jury gets to hear the right stuff."

"Oh, that's so cool," I said nodding. "That would actually be a pretty cool job," I said, thoughtfully. " I don't know anyone in the legal system, so I never even consider what goes on there."

"I guess that's a benefit of having a dad who's a lawyer."

"You could help a lot of people by being a judge—just by making sure things were fair in your courtroom."

"Yeah," he said, pulling back and smiling at me like he couldn't quite figure me out. "You look good," he said, nodding casually and changing the subject as we walked. "Thanks again. This'll help me a lot."

"It's really no problem," I said. We were getting close to the action, and I glanced around, trying to catch a glimpse of the festivities. It was quiet until we reached the area overlooking the beach. That was where the party was set up, and I could hear the noise of music playing and people talking. It grew louder as we approached.

Somehow, miraculously, I was able to be myself and not be self-conscious at all. Confidence came easily to me. I didn't know any of them, and I was pretending to be someone else, but I was able to be myself—the same relaxed Lucy my family encountered.

We sat at a table with Drew's parents, which basically meant we sat with a bunch of important people. Our table had a lot of visitors. I knew Jocelyn would've been one of them if I hadn't been there with Drew. Drew pointed her out to me, and I couldn't help but notice that she stared at us the entire time. Every time I looked at her she was staring our way. She got especially perturbed when she saw me talking to Drew's family. We were having a conversation, and I looked happy and natural around them because I was happy and natural. Jocelyn got more and more agitated throughout dinner.

CHAPTER 7

⸺⸺

*D*rew said he thought there would be a hundred people at the party, but it sure felt like more than that to me. The atmosphere was noisy and lively, even when we ate dinner. The lead singer of the band was good at keeping us all entertained. There was a small dance floor near the stage that would definitely fill up after we ate. The band was good and they played danceable classics from the sixties and seventies—the songs I had grown up listening to. I wasn't necessarily planning on getting up and dancing, but I loved hearing all of the familiar music playing while we ate and talked. We shared constant, cordial conversation all throughout dinner.

Drew was a natural politician. He could have easily run for office with his looks and personality. He might have to after a few years since some judges were elected officials. Drew was handsome, and he had impeccable manners and social skills. He shook hands and looked people in the eyes. It came out during dinner that he was twenty-four, but he carried himself with the confidence and poise of someone older.

He rarely, if ever, made physical contact with me. But he included me in the conversation, and he did things like holding my chair when we sat down. His family asked me a few questions, and I answered candidly, trying to be friendly but not give them too much personal information.

I told them I was a children's book author, which made me feel really dignified. They asked me questions about it, and I told them about the series I had been working on and the illustrator I just hired. It sounded much more glamorous than it was, which was great for both Drew and me.

I was doing fine and answering all of their questions honestly, but then they started asking me things about my family. They asked about my parents, and they were just starting to figure out that we were the owners of the local hardware store when Brian, Drew's brother-in-law, walked up and saved the day.

Drew had an older sister named Michelle. She and her husband, Brian, had been sitting at our table the whole time. I had heard them mention their two-year-old son, Blake, several times. From what I gathered, there was childcare provided at this party, but their son was having trouble staying in the room with the babysitter.

"We're just going to have to go," Brian said coming back to the table, shaking his head and wearing a frustrated expression. "He's ready to go home, Michelle. He's not having it in there."

"Just bring him out here," Drew's mom said, overhearing them.

"Seriously?" Michelle said, looking frustrated and disappointed. She stared at her mom for saying that. "He'd be all over the place out here. If he can't get it together, we'll just have to go home.

"Why don't you go in there and see if you can calm him down?" Brian suggested.

Michelle shook her head. "I've already been in there for thirty minutes while y'all were eating. The whole point is that I wanted to be here for the party. If I stay in there any more, I'll miss the whole thing."

Brian sat down next to her. "I told you we should've just had my mom watch him at home," he said.

She sighed. "Why don't they try reading him a book? There are books in his diaper bag."

"I told them about the books," Brian said, shaking his head. "I don't know what to tell you, Michelle. They asked me to tell you to go back there. He's a mess. I almost brought him out here with me so he could see you."

"Don't leave," Drew's mom said, chiming in again. "You'll miss the family picture. Just bring him out here if you need to."

I leaned forward, raising my hand a little and waving to get their attention. "I'd love to give it a shot, if you don't mind," I said.

Everyone looked at me when I spoke.

"I wouldn't mind going to hang out with Blake for a little while," I added. "I love kids."

"Thank you," Michelle said. "Really? Would you do that?"

"Sure, I don't mind at all."

I was having a fine time with everyone, and it was easy as far as fake dates went, but I wasn't in it for the date. I figured hanging out with a two-year-old could be fun.

"I'll walk you over there," Drew said.

I didn't want him to have to do that, but he didn't seem to mind. We set off for the conference room since that was where they had childcare.

"How do you think it's going?" I asked as we walked away from the party.

"Amazing," he said. "They love you. You're doing perfect." He put his arm around my shoulders as we walked out of the main area. It was a friendly gesture, but I figured it seemed more significant to anyone who was looking at us. I leaned into him. I felt certain that Jocelyn was noticing us. I felt like my mission was complete. That thought made me think of getting a ride home.

"I don't know why we didn't think of me driving here," I said, pulling back and looking at Drew. "I'm not going to be able to be here all night, and I don't want to make you leave when I do. I should've driven over here instead of leaving my car at the park."

"No, it's no big deal," Drew said, letting go of me and walking beside me. "I'll drive you home whenever you're ready."

We could hear the baby crying before we opened the door. I turned and looked at Drew. "Go back to the party," I said.

"Tell your sister I'll come get her if we need her, but otherwise he's fine."

"She'll assume he's fine. If we don't go back out there, she'll know we're taking care of it."

"I got it," I said. "You go back."

"Do you really think you can stop that?" He squinted like his ears were hurting and pointed toward the door, indicating the sound of the crying toddler.

"Yes," I said. I opened the door. "I'm going in."

"I'm coming with you!" he said, comically following me as if we were going into battle.

"Enter at your own risk," I said, shaking my head at him."

The sound got louder with every step we took. He was an older toddler, I could tell by his voice, and he was not happy.

"How are you going to fix this?" Drew asked.

"I know what to do. I'm about to need a hero. We'll see if he can step up to a challenge."

"Okay, let's see what you got," Drew said with a nod as we entered the room.

Another round of wails rang out, and he flinched comically at the sound. There were two large conjoined rooms, and probably twenty kids spread out throughout both of them but Blake was the only one who was bawling, so it was easy to figure out who he was.

I didn't stop walking until we got right up to him. I made eye contact with the girl, the hired babysitter, who was holding him. I reached out for him, and she gladly handed him over.

"Oh, my goodness, are you Blake?"

I held him close, comforting him and speaking quietly, making myself sound vulnerable and a little like I was in a hurry. I walked into the corner of the room, moving slowly and swaying gently with him in my arms.

"My name is Lucy. I'm here with your Uncle Drew, he's right here with me. You can see him. Hey, Blake, I could really use your help on a mission. Drew was telling me you're really brave and smart, and I need some help. Can you help me find something special, please, something that I lost?"

I was speaking with enough quiet urgency that my intention cut through his crying fit. He became quieter, gasping for air as he contemplated what I was saying. He picked his head up, looking at Drew as if checking to see if my story checked out. He started to wiggle in my arms in a way that let me know he was about to begin having a fit again.

"Oh, please, you're my only hope, Blake. I've got to find my lost rock! Can you please help me if we walk outside? It was really smooth, and it was just my favorite rock in the whole world. I need it for my pocket. I lost it right outside. Could you help me find it, please? I'll make you a deal. If you can help me find my lucky rock, I'll give you a sucker. Can he have a sucker?" I added, speaking to Drew, who nodded.

Blake relaxed a little, staring at me. I could tell he knew what I was saying when I offered candy. He looked at Drew for confirmation and Drew nodded again. "If she knows where to get one," Drew said.

"I have one in my purse," I said. "Multiple. I know I have grape. I might have a cherry and orange, too. I usually have a bunch in there. Do you want to look and see what colors I have?"

Blake pulled back, searching me for the stash. He was still gasping, but he had calmed down considerably.

"How about this... let me set you down. We can look in my purse. I'll let you pick out a sucker, and then we'll go outside and you can help me find my rock."

He nodded, but he was still shaken from that fit, and he took gasps of air, breathing three or four of them in a row. Drew just stood back and watched us quietly. I was glad he was there because it made Blake trust me. There were other kids around, but they had been flocking to the other side of the room on account of Blake's screaming, and no one was anywhere near us. I got situated beside Blake and gingerly pulled four suckers out of my purse. I intentionally worked slowly so that he could compose himself.

"There's a root beer, a cherry, and two grapes," I said, holding them out. "I knew there would be a grape," I added. "You know why?" I paused, looking at Blake.

"Why?" he said. (Gasp, gasp, gasp.)

"Because I saw it in there earlier. It's my favorite flavor, so I always look for it." I smiled at him and held the lollipops in my palm for him to choose one. Of course, he chose the cherry. I knew he would.

"I like cherry too," I said. I held it close to his pocket like I was trying to help him hide it. "Hold onto it," I added, whispering and looking around. "Put it in your pocket, so the other kids can't see, and save it for when we get outside. I would share with everyone, but I don't think I have enough." I helped him get it into his pocket as I continued speaking. "Listen, we'll go outside. You can eat your sucker, and I'll tell you a story while we look for my rock. I know a really good story about a bear and a turtle who made friends."

Aside from some sporadic, almost silent gasps, Blake had completely stopped crying. We waved at the babysitters, checking in with them on our way out, but they were so relieved to have the crying stopped that they just smiled and waved at us.

We left the kids' room, heading in the opposite direction of the party. I looked at Drew right when we made it outside. "Blake and I can take it from here," I said. "We'll just be a few minutes."

His smile faded. "Am I not invited?" he asked.

"No, yeah," I winked. "But I think Blake can help me with the rock if you want to get back to your dad."

Blake was walking beside me contentedly, and I stooped and took the sucker out of his pocket. I unwrapped it and handed it to him.

"Well, if it'll only take a minute, then I'll stay," Drew said.

It took us five minutes to "find my rock" and during that time, I told Blake about the turtle and the bear. I made it up on the spot, and it wasn't my best work, but it was zany enough for a two-year-old to enjoy. The story ended with a race where the turtle held onto wheels and the bear rode on the turtle's back like a skateboard. I did silly voices, and Blake was cracking up by the time we found my rock.

Blake was exponentially more reasonable once he was in a good mood. I told him this night was a big deal for his grandfather and that we needed to get out there with the adults for just a little while.

I told him if he let one of those teachers read him a story, it would be over in no time. I let him hang on to my special rock until his parents got back, and I gave him a second sucker for being so helpful, but we put that one in his diaper bag and we said he'd save it for later.

He was fine when we left. He was holding the rock and sitting down for a book. The whole ordeal took about ten minutes.

Drew and I made eye contact when we left the children's area. I stopped walking, hesitating in the hall.

"Aren't you coming back?" he asked, gesturing toward the party.

I shrugged. "Don't you think you made your point? I think everybody got the idea that you're with someone else."

"So, you're leaving? You're going home?"

"My mom's friend actually lives pretty close to here. That's where Mac is. I could just walk over there. It'll only take me a few minutes, and she can take me to my car."

"I'll take you to your car if you need to leave now," he said.

"No, no, I've already taken you away from the party long enough. You should go back in. I'm fine walking over there, actually."

"In a skirt? Just stay a little longer," he said, reaching out, touching my arm. "Come back in there with me. Seriously, it's helping me out a lot. She's gonna be all over me if you leave."

I glanced in the direction of the party. I could hear the music faintly.

"I could stay another half-hour," I said.

Drew smiled and took a hold of me, lacing my hand through his arm and forcing me to hold onto his arm as we walked. I didn't resist. He was a smart, rich, handsome Senator's son, and his arm had muscles. He was fun to hold onto. *How many times in life would I get to live this kind of fairy tale situation?*

Drew leaned in to speak to me as we walked to the covered cabana area where the party was set up. He joked about me being Lady Lollipop from the dock, and how fitting it was that

I actually carried lollipops around with me. We were smiling about it as we entered the party area. People looked at us. I could feel them staring. But I just talked to Drew, feeling calm and happy.

I decided that fake dates were the best kind of dates. There was no pressure. I could just be myself and not worry about impressing the guy I was with. I didn't even really feel like I needed to impress his family or friends. This was the best possible date. I was myself, and at the same time, I was being someone else.

"What are you thinking," Drew asked smiling at me as we approached our table.

"Just about this night."

"What are you thinking about it?"

"I don't know. I'm just glad I came here. It's a cool experience."

"Good. I'm glad you didn't leave."

He glanced around, evaluating our surroundings before we sat down. "Would you like to dance?" he asked.

And since going with the flow seemed to be working for me tonight, I said, "Sure."

CHAPTER 8

*D*rew readjusted his grip on me, taking a hold of my hand instead of my arm. I tried not to notice the bodily sensations I got from holding his touch. He gently tugged me along, and I followed him. I assumed we were going to the dance floor, since that was what he had just mentioned, but he went to our table. He went straight to his sister and stood behind her.

"Blake's doing great, thanks to Lucy," he said when she looked back at him.

Michelle shifted, staring at me with a surprised expression "What? Really? Is he fine?"

"You just have to know how to look for lucky rocks and tell stories about skateboarding bears."

"Huh?" Michelle said.

But Drew was backing up already, and he was pulling me with him. "Nothing," he called, smiling. "Blake's good, though. He's happy."

"Thank you!" she said, waving at us.

Others at Drew's table noticed us going to the dance floor and came out there as well. We danced to a song called *Shake Rattle and Roll*, and then a slower one called *Only the Lonely*. Drew held me like it was a slow dance for that one. He led the entire time, moving me how he pleased, and leaving me no other choice but to be a good dancer.

It was fun being led by him. I just let myself be pulled along, and I got to take the credit for us looking good out there.

The lead singer spoke to the crowd between songs. "All right, we have one more, and then we're going to take a minute and hear from the birthday boy," he said.

Everyone cheered. I glanced at Drew, who was standing next to me. We had broken apart when the band stopped playing. "I might slip out," I said when they started up again.

Drew glanced over my shoulder, making a worried expression. "Hang on, I need to do this," he said. He stepped closer to me, leaning down. And one swift motion his face came closer and closer to mine, and the next thing I knew, his lips were on mine. He kissed me. He did it twice, taking me into his arms as he kissed me gently. I forgot to breathe. I just went with it and kissed him back.

The band began playing a medium-tempo song. It was groovy from the first few notes, and my encounter with Drew matched with the music in a way that made my blood run hot. His kiss was gentle, but it was scorching, and I felt breathless and boneless when he broke it.

Thankfully, he didn't let go of me. He held me close dancing, swaying.

"Thank you," he said near my ear, holding me, dancing with me in his arms.

"You're welcome," I said after a few seconds of stunned silence. "Was your girlfriend coming or something?"

"Ex, and yeah."

"I figured," I whispered, nodding and trying to get myself together.

"My dad will only talk for a few minutes," Drew said. "I'll drive you to your friend's house after that. Or back to get your car. I'll take you anywhere you want to go." Drew swayed to the rhythm as he spoke, leading me. He was so calm. *How was he so calm?*

"Yeah, that's fine," I said, nodding. I swayed with him to the rhythm. It was one of my favorite songs. It was called *Time After Time*, and it was originally sung by Cyndi Lauper. I had never heard a guy sing it, and he was doing an amazing job. I loved it. Maybe that was just because I was so out of it from that unexpected kiss.

But really, it wasn't that unexpected. I was supposed to be his girlfriend, after all. I rested my face against his shirt, feeling thankful for the ability to hide behind him while I was feeling vulnerable and shaken. The lead singer had a higher voice that went well with this song.

After my picture fades
And darkness has turned to gray,
Watching through windows,
You're wondering if I'm okay.
Secrets stolen from deep inside
The drum beats out of time...

The band performed the chorus two more times, and Drew held me and danced with me until the end. By the time we were done on the dance floor, I was physically different than when we went out there. I felt like I was a soda that had been shaken up and now I was weak in the knees and distracted, decarbonated if you will.

Fake date, fake date, fake date.

You are on a fake date.

I repeated the mantra, reminding myself of that since I didn't want to get carried away. I smiled and stood up straight and went to the job of being the girlfriend of the Senator's son.

Andrew Klein made a speech. In it, he mentioned Drew—how proud he was that Drew had finished law school and would be practicing soon. He talked about his wife and daughter, and said how proud and happy he was to have such a wonderful support system as he tried his best to represent the great state of Texas. He went on about what a wonderful place we called home. Everyone loved it when he complimented Texas.

When he finished, Drew and I walked toward our table. Drew told his family I was leaving, and they made a bigger deal about it than I thought they would.

His family protested, but I told them I had to go. They offered to have a driver take me home if I needed to leave, but Drew insisted that he wanted to do it. He said he would come back to the party in a little while.

For a moment, I felt torn, like I didn't want to leave the party. But then I remembered that was ludicrous. I was doing this as a favor. I was happy to be leaving. I needed to get back to my life.

We were quiet during the first minute or so after we got into his Bronco.

"We used to stop at this place off the interstate called Stuckey's," he said, finally.

"I know Stuckey's," I said. "My little brothers and I used to always beg my parents to let us buy this plastic switch-blade comb they had in the souvenir section. They had tons of little trinkets like that. In fact, I think that's where Mac got that coon skin cap he had on when we met. It was Phillip's."

"I remember that switchblade comb," Drew said. "I had one of those things."

"My parents wouldn't let us get one. They said someone might see it from a distance and get the wrong idea. We were little, though. I haven't been in a Stuckey's in a long time."

Drew smiled and nodded. "I loved that place. I haven't been to one in a long time either, but I have this comfortable, nostalgic feeling when I think about it. That's what I feel like around you. Like Stuckey's."

"What?" I said, smiling.

"I don't know. I feel like Stuckey's around you."

I looked at him from over the console, smiling and shaking my head.

"What? It's true. That whole thing with Blake, I guess. It was just cool and comforting, watching you do your thing and tell that story to him. It was fun and different. It was nostalgic."

"Like Stuckey's?" I asked.

"Yeah," he said, smiling.

"I'll take that as a compliment."

"You should," he said, nodding with certainty. "It was one. It was amazing to see you get everything under control like that. Your personality… it's like some kind of ointment."

"Ointment?" I asked, laughing.

"You know what I mean," he said. "You come around, and it's like so… it's easy to be around you, that's all. Comfortable. You're weird. You're wise. I can't tell if you're like… eighteen or eighty."

I smiled. "I feel like you're trying to compliment me right now," I said, teasing him.

"I am," he said, nodding.

"Well, as long as we're paying compliments, you have a wonderful family." I paused, but then added, "And you're really good at interacting with everybody. I had a lot of fun tonight. I have to say, I enjoyed this fake date better than any real date I've ever been on."

I was being lighthearted, but I got nervous because I had a flashback of what he did to me on the dancefloor. Because of this, I switched to a fake British accent when I said that last part about enjoying the fake date. It was such a bad accent that I had to do a little voice with it just to distract. I really hoped he didn't think I was thinking about the kiss so I continued babbling.

"...I just didn't know what I was getting into when I met you at the dock tonight. A Senator's birthday party was not what I expected, and I had fun, that's all. Thank you."

"I didn't think you'd come," he said. "I thought maybe that lady at the hardware store wouldn't even tell you I came by."

"She didn't," I said. "Someone overheard you and told me about it behind her back."

"You're kidding!" he said.

"No," I said, laughing a little.

"This whole evening hinged on eavesdropping?"

"Yes," I said, laughing. "It actually did."

I stopped talking and pointed out of the front windshield when I saw my car in the distance. I had been giving him directions to get to my car since he had come to me by boat earlier.

"It's the red car right there," I said, pointing at my little Honda hatchback.

Drew pulled up behind me. His Bronco was lifted up on these high tires, and it seemed like we could just drive right over my car and clear it. It wasn't even close to that, but I still smiled at the thought.

"What?" he asked, glancing at me.

"I was thinking of driving over my car," I said. "You know, just making a tunnel over it. I imagined us being tall enough to do that."

"You imagine a lot of things," he said.

"Yeah," I said, laughing a little at how true that statement was. "You imagined I was Stuckey's, though," I said. He was in the middle of laughing at that when I reached for my door handle. "I know you need to rush back, but thank you for everything. Thanks again for inviting me. That was fun-n... no, actually..." I stared at him with wide eyes when I remembered something.

"What?" he asked.

"Can I change right here in your truck real quick before I get out? This is so much bigger than my car, and I should probably be wearing jeans when I get back to Evelyn's. Would you stand right outside and look that way for just a second while I do this really quick? Is that too much to ask?"

"Of course not," Drew said. He got out of his truck. He left it running with the front headlights on, and he went to the front of the truck and turned the other way where the light was shining on his back. I glanced at him a few times while I changed, but he never looked back, and I was done quickly.

I folded the skirt carelessly and shoved it back into my purse before heading outside to say goodnight to Drew.

CHAPTER 9

"Thank you," I said.

"That was quick," he said. He turned to look at me, smiling when I came into the light. "Nice jeans."

I smiled and did a goofy pose where I made finger guns. "Thanks." I kept smiling at him, but I was walking, going to my car.

"Oh, you're leaving that fast?" he said.

"I was just trying to let you go. I figured both of us need to get back to our stuff."

"Okay, well, can you come over here and say goodbye to me? If we're going to finish our fake date, we might as well have a fake goodbye."

"Okay," I said, feeling suddenly nervous.

I walked over to him, and he reached out and hugged me. It wasn't awkward at all. He was confident and happy, and I couldn't help but smile as we hugged. Just then, I saw headlights coming down the street. It was not a busy road, so I took two steps back from Drew instinctually.

Thank goodness I did, because seconds later, I noticed that the approaching vehicle was my dad's truck. He pulled up quickly, and he stopped near us and got out. We were standing in the light, and I had broken the hug in plenty of time that I didn't think my dad had even seen us. There was nothing to hide, but I couldn't help but feel like I'd been caught. I warned Drew that it was my dad.

"What are you doing?" Dad asked, coming around the front of his truck after he parked.

"I went to Drew's dad's birthday party. This is my friend, Drew. Drew Klein," I said, gesturing to him.

Dad hesitated, giving Drew a once-over before thoughtfully sticking his hand out for a handshake. "Daniel King," Dad said. "I'm Lucy's father."

They shook hands like gentlemen, but neither of them was smiling.

Dad looked at me. "Mom and I didn't know where you were."

"I didn't mention it because I didn't want you to worry. But I'm fine. I worked it out with Evelyn. She's watching Mac. I was just about to go over there and get him."

"Okay, well, we put the pieces together and figured this was where you'd come. I just wanted to come over here and make sure you are okay." Dad seemed like he was going to leave us be, but he was still taking in my surroundings.

"I'm fine," I said. "Thank you for coming here. Thank you for checking on me. I'm sorry I didn't mention it."

"All right," Dad said, nodding and backing off while still checking out Drew. "Are you coming home now?"

"Yes sir. I have to stop at Evelyn's and pick up Mac, but I'll be home after."

"Okay, then," Dad said, walking toward his truck again. "Good to meet you Drew Klein," he added.

He drove away, and I waited to make sure he was out of possible earshot before I spoke again. I breathed a sigh, smiling.

"Sooo, that was my dad," I said.

"Yeah," Drew agreed. "Was he upset?"

"No, they were probably just worried. He knew about that message you left me at the store today, and he didn't tell me about it, so I'm sure he figured everything out and got worried." I smiled broadly at him. "I was tempted to tell Dad it was a fake date because I knew that would ease his mind, but it would've taken too long to explain and I know you need to go."

I waved with my keys in my hand as I walked away. Drew smiled and waved at me too, but I could tell he was a little disappointed, like he wanted to say something else. I figured he didn't know what to think about my dad driving up on us.

I put one foot in front of the other, going to my car, ignoring the fact that I had gotten all stirred up inside thinking that he might kiss me. Dad's appearance had broken the trance I was in, but my body still felt that yearning sensation like our goodbye was missing something.

I should have just done it. I should've just kissed him after my dad drove away. Drew would've been fine with that, I knew he would have by the way he was looking at me. He would've kissed me back.

But it was too late to worry about it now. I had already been kissed once this evening, which was more than I expected and more than had happened in years.

I smiled at the thought of what happened on the dancefloor. I was daydreaming about it as I put my car in drive.

I was just about to pull away when I heard Drew honk his horn. I wasn't expecting the loud noise, and it startled me. I stared in my rearview mirror, wondering if I should stop or if he was just honking to say goodbye. I had to squint into the reflection of his headlights, but I saw his driver's door open.

I put my car in park and got out to go meet him. I was in a swimmy, dreamlike state, giddy and full of butterflies as I approached the too-handsome man. I wanted to be next to him. I was pulled to him like there was a gravitational force between us.

I just knew he was getting out of the truck to kiss me. We both knew this opportunity was too good to pass up. *How many times in life could you blame a reckless kiss on a fake date scenario?* This never happened. We should take advantage of it. We obviously had to. He had honked and gotten out of his truck, after all.

I walked toward him, feeling excited, expectant.

"Your lantern," he said, smiling as he walked toward me. It took a second for me to register what he was saying, and by that time, my momentum had carried me to where he was standing. We stopped with only a couple of feet between us. The light was at his back, so his face was in a shadow. I blinked up at him. "Thanks," I said, feeling utterly let down but trying not to show it.

"Or I guess it might be Mac's," he said, lifting the lantern.

"Yeah, yeah," I said nervously. I reached out and took the lantern from him, trying not to notice that our fingers touched during the transfer. "Thank you," I said. "I'm glad you caught me. He would have been looking for this."

"Lucy."

"Yeah?"

He reached out for me, and I was so ready for it to happen that I went toward him. He put his arms loosely around me, hesitating from only inches away, staring.

My. Heart. Was. Pounding.

I swallowed and blinked up at him, and the next thing I knew, he ducked and kissed me.

Drew Klein, the Senator's son, kissed me right here with nobody watching. It was a closed-mouth kiss, but it was tender, and he held it there long enough that his lips molded to mine.

Drew was amazing.

I hadn't kissed a man in a long time, and even then, it had not been this good. He kissed me slowly, carefully, like he wanted me to enjoy it.

He kissed me five or six times, administering light, guttingling kisses that had me experiencing waves of endorphins. My body was electrified. Drew had a hold of my arms, but I didn't even notice until he used his grip on me to push me back a little and break the kiss.

"Oh, Lu, girl, one more, please." He leaned in and kissed me again. "Goodness." He kissed me twice more. "Stop it," he said.

"You're the one doin—" I couldn't even finish my sentence because he kissed me again. He kept kissing me lightly for another full minute before he finally pulled back.

"Okay, we have to go," he said. "Gosh."

"Yes, we do," I agreed. And I put my words into action by stepping out of his grasp and beginning to walk away. I smiled at him and waved. I was dazed, but I did my best to act normal.

"Thanks for the lantern," I said, like a big dork.

"You're welcome," he said.

I took a few steps toward my car.

"When will I see you again?" he asked.

"You're looking at me right now," I called, smiling.

"I'm serious!" he yelled.

I lifted my hands and made an exaggerated shrugging motion. "You know where I work."

"I'll call you!" he yelled while I was already in the process of getting into my car.

"Okay!" I yelled back.

I was acting unaffected, but my body was absolutely reeling from that kiss. My mind was racing. Everything Drew just did was exactly what I wanted to happen, but I honestly didn't know what to think about it or what to do from here. I could easily fall for Drew, but in my heart, I knew that wasn't an option. *Or was it? Could it be possible that he would want something more than just a casual relationship with me?*

I thought of Mac.

I went through the process of getting back into my car and stashing the lantern, thinking of my life and how unlikely the odds were that someone like Drew would ever be able to fall for someone like me. I wasn't trying to be down on myself. I loved Mac, and I had no regrets. But I knew Drew's family would have felt differently about him "dating" me if they knew I already had a child.

My kiss-induced bliss was interrupted somewhat by my hopeless thoughts. I told myself to let go of it and enjoy the moment for what it was. It had been an amazing night.

I saw a shadow caused by something in front of his headlights, and I turned just in time to see Drew approaching my side of the car. I gave him a curious expression through the window, but he just smiled at me and reached down to open the door. I felt vulnerable sitting there with him staring down at me with my car door open.

"What?" I said when he just stood there for a few seconds. "You better get back to that party," I added, smiling at him.

"I wish you could come back with me," he said.

I shook my head, still smiling. "I would, but I have to go pick up Mac and get him home. Back to reality."

"This is reality, too," he said.

I started to speak but then hesitated, closing my mouth and not knowing the proper response to that statement.

"When can I see you again?" he asked.

I was so surprised by his persistence that I said, "I don't know."

"Tomorrow?"

"Uh, sure," I said, sounding uncertain.

"What's the matter?"

"Nothing," I said. "I was just thinking, tomorrow's Sunday. We were planning on eating lunch at my aunt's house after church, and then I just have Mac after that, so… I didn't know what you were thinking, but… "

"Should I eat lunch with you at your aunt's? Can I? Is it Billy Castro's house, or your other aunt? I've been wanting to meet your uncle."

(I had told him during one of our earlier conversations that the famous boxer, "Easy" Billy Castro, was my uncle, so he was correct to assume that was where I was going for lunch.)

"Yeah, it's at their house, and you can come if you want. But it's just my family. Nothing fancy."

"I don't need fancy," he said. "Could you take a second and write down the address and phone number, please."

"Sure," I said.

I was so surprised by his persistent interest that I felt shaken. I was almost sure he could tell I was shaking as I wrote down the information he needed. I handed it to him, trying my best not to shake—holding paper always made it so obvious.

"The stuff on top is my information, and the bottom is my aunt's," I said, distracting him. "I guess if you were just going to meet us for lunch, you don't really need my address, but... anyway. Those are our addresses and my phone number."

"Where's this phone number lead to? Your parents' house?"

"No, no, to my house. Me and Mac. In the back. They don't pick up that phone... unless they're at my house. But, no, that's my phone."

"Okay," he said "What time tomorrow?"

"Twelve-thirty or one," I said. "You do know my dad's going to be there, right?"

"Yes. Why? Should I be scared of your dad?"

"Not if we're just friends," I said, smiling. "None of this fake boyfriend stuff at my house."

He grinned. "Okay. I'll just be your friend tomorrow. I'll see you then."

CHAPTER 10

There were seven of us cousins. I had more in my extended family, but there were seven of us who stayed close and got together frequently. I was the oldest, but the rest of them were not much younger than me. Counting the aunts, uncles, grandparents, and friends, there would be around twenty of us at lunch today.

Tess and Billy had two kids named Tara and Will. My parents had myself, Phillip, and Evan.

And my Aunt Laney (on my dad's side) had twins named Jenny and Josh.

We all met at Tess and Billy's after church for lunch. It wasn't something that happened every Sunday, but we tried to get together for birthdays, and sometimes we would just default to the nearest Sunday to celebrate since it was a time when most of us could make time to do it.

That was what was happening this week. Three people, including myself, had birthdays recently, so it was time we all got together and had a family lunch.

I hadn't heard from Drew, so I had no idea if he was planning on coming or not. But he did. It was close to 1pm when he arrived. My cousin heard him at the door and let him in. We had just called everyone to the kitchen to pray and make our plates. I was standing on the other side of the room when Drew came around the corner, and I made a quick introduction from afar.

My mom, who was standing next to Drew, reached out and gave him a sideways hug. My family was full of huggers, and Drew didn't hesitate to receive two or three of them from nearby women. He also shook a few hands of guys who were standing nearby. It all happened really quickly.

I was on the other side of the kitchen, holding Mac on my hip. My mom and aunt talked to Drew. I couldn't hear them, and I really hoped they weren't making him feel on the spot like they thought he was my boyfriend. He was smiling every time I glanced over there, so I assumed it was fine. I hoped it was.

My aunt had cooked pork roast and rice and gravy with potato casserole and several other vegetables, including my aunt's famous fried eggplant straws. Mac loved those. It was the only way he would eat eggplant. He was working on one of them at the moment.

My Uncle Billy said a few things about the birthdays we had celebrated, and I smiled and did a little bow when he announced my name and everyone cheered. I made eye contact with Drew briefly after that, and I had to work at keeping my expression neutral.

I just loved how he looked. He was physically strong and sturdy. That was why I had fallen so hard for Bradley. Drew was athletic, and I was drawn to that in men. It seemed that male muscles were my kryptonite. The sight of Drew Klein standing in my aunt's kitchen made my heart beat faster.

Because of Drew's timing, and the way we were all standing in the crowded kitchen, I didn't end up next to him for the first minute or two.

Finally, after about half of the people in the kitchen finished serving themselves and made their way out, Drew and I were able to converge.

I couldn't believe he was here. He was seeing me in my natural habitat, with Mac on my hip. I was almost scared to go up to him. All I could think about was kissing him the night before, and I didn't want him to know it was on my mind or think that I assumed it meant something. I didn't even know what I was assuming. My thoughts were jumbled, shifting, choppy. He was coming over to me.

"Hey," he said.

"Hey."

"Hello, Mac."

"Hey. Hi, Mister Drew," he said, correcting himself since he knew I would do it.

"Hello, Mister Mac," Drew said.

Mac wiggled and reached out for my mom who came up from the side of me.

"I'll take him while you guys eat," she said. "We'll go get some more of Aunt Tess's eggplant."

I got in line behind my cousin, Tara, and Drew followed me. I showed him the ropes of the buffet, and we served ourselves. Tara asked Drew where he was from, and then others chimed in, and in that conversation, it came out that he was the Senator's son. I got a few conspiratorial looks from family members, asking me if I was interested in him, but no one made it obvious. They all treated him like he was my friend, which was a relief to me.

Drew seemed relaxed and was being his easy-going self. More than once, during the course of the afternoon, he pretended to get hurt in some funny way for Mac's entertainment.

My family was laidback, and Drew was cool enough to fit in like he had always been a part of it. He talked to everyone, and they talked to him. They discussed boxing, lawyering, owning a hardware store, and all the other things they did on a daily basis.

It came out that Drew's parents owned a house in Galveston. I knew he had spent the night here, but it didn't fully register because he kept referring to it as "the camp" so I wasn't quite sure that he was going to an actual house. Drew explained where it was, and we were all familiar with the neighborhood. His family had a beachfront home that was up on high piers.

I had a friend who lived in that neighborhood when I was growing up, so I had been there a lot.

I said I was surprised I didn't run into him before, and he said that his parents only bought it a couple of years ago, when they heard about the construction of Palm Beach.

Drew was the center of most of the conversation at lunch. I was the oldest, and Drew was a few years older than me, so all of my cousins were enamored with him. My parents seemed to like him, too.

We spent a while eating and visiting before a few people mentioned that they needed to leave. Because of that, we decided to go ahead and sing and eat the birthday cake. The dining room was filled past capacity when we gathered around the table to sing the birthday song.

Some were standing but Drew and I were sitting at the table, shoved in close to everybody else. There were so many extra chairs around the table that we basically created one long curved bench instead of separate chairs. I was close enough to Drew that the side of my leg was touching his. I tried not to notice, but it was impossible.

My uncle mentioned the three people who were celebrating a birthday and said the song was meant for all of us. They sang, and people looked all around, smiling at each other. I liked that I wasn't the only one celebrating a birthday. It made me feel better that it wasn't all eyes on me. Even still, I felt a little shy as they sang.

I was smiling when I performed the nervous, absentminded gesture of rubbing my own thighs. I didn't even mean to do it, but without thinking, I just slowly ran my hands from my hips toward my knees.

There was so much chaos and noise in the room that no one saw my fingertips touch the side of Drew's leg. I hadn't meant to touch him, and the contact surprised me. I kept my hand on my own leg, but I quickly moved it where I was no longer touching Drew's. I wasn't sure if my heart was racing because of the birthday song or from my proximity to Drew. I smiled, looking around casually at everyone. All of this was happening in the span of seconds while the song was being sung.

There was a big, loud, jumbled bunch of words when we got to the part in the song where you were supposed to say the name of the birthday boy or girl. Some people said one name, some people said another, most people tried to fit in all three names in a row. It got really chaotic for a few seconds when that happened, and everyone laughed afterward. It was during that chaos that Drew reached over and took my hand. It was the same hand I had touched him with a few seconds earlier.

My hand was still resting on my leg when Drew very intentionally put his hand over it. For a few seconds there, I didn't remember to breathe. They finished that last line that says *happy birthday to you*, and everyone clapped.

He took his hand away to do that, but he had definitely been touching me under the table. For several seconds there, he was officially holding my hand. A couple of other times after that, Drew and I bumped into each other or held eye contact for longer than normal, but the intentional contact during the birthday song was the only official PDA that had occurred— and even then, it was under the table, so it wasn't very public. It was an intentional hand-holding, though. It was sincere. He had rubbed my hand with his thumb.

I was thinking about it as I stood at my aunt's kitchen sink and rinsed out a cup for Mac. I snapped to attention when I heard the sound of Mac crying from a distance, and I braced myself, not knowing what I would see when he came into the kitchen.

Drew had been on the porch with my cousins, but he came inside holding Mac who was crying.

"He's okay," Drew said. "Just a skinned knee. He tripped on the sidewalk."

Mac was crying loudly. Drew's voice was calm, but it cut through the sound. I took Mac from him wondering why someone in my family hadn't been the one to take Mac. I didn't want Drew to have to deal with him when he was like this.

"Listen, it's okay," I said. "Your mama's a professional at skinned knees, remember? I'll have it bandaged with medicine and feeling better in no time."

Mac nodded, still crying but getting better now that I wasn't alarmed.

"Thank you for getting him to the hospital, Mister Drew. I'm Doctor Mama, and I do believe he's going to be just fine from this. I'll have him up and running again in no time."

I set Mac on the counter. It was a move we did all the time. He was old enough by now to know not to jump down by himself. I left him there and dug in a nearby cabinet where I knew my aunt kept her first aid supplies.

Within a minute, Mac was bandaged up and heading outside with my mother who came in while I was tending to his knee.

"Sorry," I said, once Drew and I were alone in the kitchen.

"Sorry for what?" Drew asked.

"For that. I didn't mean to put you on first aid duty when I came inside."

"I wanted to be on first aid duty," Drew said. "I was just happy he came to me. I didn't think he would do that. Did I do something wrong? Why didn't you want me on duty?"

I let out a little laugh. "No, no you did great."

I was going to add that I was sorry about him having to deal with the responsibility of a crying baby, but then I decided not to say it. Drew didn't seem to mind helping out, anyway.

"We'll probably leave in the next twenty minutes," I said instead. "Jenny's coming over to the house so we can help her make those cookies."

Drew had overheard the conversation where Aunt Laney's daughter, my cousin Jenny, asked Mom and me if we would help her bake cookies for a cheerleading bake sale. She knew my mom loved to bake and that we had two kitchens to get it done faster.

"Oh, okay," Drew said, nodding.

We were silent for a few seconds. There were people in adjoining rooms, and we could hear them talking, but he and I were alone in the kitchen. He was wearing an easy smile, but I had no idea what he was thinking.

"Unless you want to come over and help with the cookies," I said.

His smile broadened. "I'd love to."

CHAPTER 11

Drew

*D*rew stared at his own reflection in the bathroom mirror. He was in Lucy's house—in her small bathroom. He had already been over at her mom's house, making boatloads of cookie dough with her mom and cousin.

He and Lucy took a portion of the dough to her cottage so they could bake a few batches in her oven and get it done faster. Drew had been introduced to the wiener dog, Sport, and then to the hedgehogs.

It was 5pm, and he had been with Lucy all afternoon. He felt sick at the thought of leaving her. She needed his help in life. He wanted to help her. He needed her help in life, too. *Uhhhhhh.* Her bathroom was small, and if it wasn't so close to everything, he would have been talking to himself out loud, trying to get a grip.

Drew stared at the mirror, looking into his own eyes and wondering what in the world had come over him. He had dated enough women over the years to know how to pace himself and take things slowly.

But Lucy wasn't even in the same category as other girls. He didn't just want to speed things up with her, he wanted to go full-throttle. He wanted to jump in straight away, today, and become a part of her life, part of her family.

He had been interacting with Mac all afternoon, and he knew in his heart that he would be a good father to that boy. He wanted to go back out there and beg Lucy to marry him. He was in love with the way she saw things in life—the way she carried herself—the way she affected those around her. She was innocent and naïve yet wise and totally in control.

He thought about the worlds of woodland creatures she dreamed up in those children's books, and he honestly felt like if he didn't marry this girl and become a part of everything she had going on, he would never forgive himself.

Drew took a deep calming breath, staring at his reflection, and begging himself inwardly to take it easy. He owed it to both of them to take things slowly.

Drew noticed that Lucy was on the telephone when he came back into the living room. She spoke in such a way that he assumed she was talking to her mom. She stared at him when she hung up the phone.

"Don't feel like you have to say 'yes'," was the first thing she said.

"To what?" Drew asked.

"Mom and Jenny have so much extra cookie dough up there that they were wondering if maybe you could take the rest of it over to Aunt Tess and Uncle Billy so they can bake some of it at their house.

"I don't mind at all," Drew said. "Do I need to stay while they cook it, or just drop it off?"

"No, no, nothing like that. Just drop it off."

He looked at Mac. He was a precious, dark-haired boy, and he currently had red cheeks from running around so much. He was settled down now, playing with some trucks.

"Do you want to ride over there with me?" Drew asked.

Mac looked at his mother who shrugged like she was okay with it.

"Yeah, I do. Is it gonna be in your big truck?" Mac asked.

"Yes, it is," Drew said. "Would you like to ride with me?"

Mac nodded, not looking reluctant at all.

"You have to get strapped in," Lucy said.

Drew looked at her. "Does he know how to stay with me when we get out and stuff? Is he going to listen to me? He's not going to run out into the street or anything, is he?"

Lucy looked straight at Mac with a serious, motherly stare when Drew asked that. "Are you going to listen to Mister Drew?"

"Yes ma'am."

And within minutes, Drew was driving down the street with a curious toddler and three pounds of cookie dough. He and Mac talked about fishing on the way to Tess and Billy's house, and the conversation continued when they went inside.

Tess was a painter, and she was working, so Billy was given the job of baking cookies. Drew and Mac stood in the kitchen with him while he scooped the first batch onto a cookie sheet and put it into the oven.

They spoke about fishing at first and then went on to talk about other things. Drew had seen Billy fight lots of times on television and even once in person. It had been a few years since Billy had retired, but Drew was old enough to remember his heyday. He had talked to her whole family earlier, but it was honestly a little surreal to be standing in Billy Castro's kitchen watching him bake cookies.

After a few minutes of conversation, Drew said that he and Mac needed to be going. He was relieved when Mac nodded like he was going to listen to Drew when he said it was time to go.

They had talked so long that Billy was taking the cookies out of the oven just as they were leaving. He asked if Drew could drop a few of the warm cookies off at Marvin Jones's apartment. It was just down Bank Street, above the boxing gym, and Billy said that Marvin would love getting the cookies.

Marvin Jones was a boxing legend from way back, about fifty years ago. Drew had heard of him and knew he was Billy's coach and had owned the gym before Billy took it over. Marvin did some kind of shuffling shadowboxing move back in the day. Drew's dad used to do it when Drew was a little boy.

He and Mac delivered the cookies, and Marvin was excited to get them. He was a nice man, and Drew enjoyed meeting him. Drew introduced himself as 'Lucy's friend', and Marvin told him he needed to come to the gym to work out sometime. Billy had already told him the same thing. Drew thanked Marvin for the invitation and promised that he would come back to the gym soon.

Drew and Mac were walking from the gym to the car when Mac said, "They got milkshakes in there." He pointed to the diner on the corner. Carson's.

Drew gestured to it. "Did you want to go in there and get a milkshake?"

"Sure!" Mac said, like it was all Drew's idea.

The two of them walked down the sidewalk and into Carson's Diner. It was almost dinner time, but it was Sunday, so they weren't busy. There were empty stools at the counter, and Drew and Mac took a seat there.

Mac knew just what to do, and Drew followed him. He was too short for the stool, but easily climbed up onto it without help, and he made quick work of getting settled at the counter.

"Well, hey, Mister Mac," said the cook who could see them through the window. "I didn't even recognize you at first, with your new friend."

"Yeah," Mac said, his feet swinging under the counter.

Drew glanced at the cook. "I'm Drew."

"Patrick," the cook replied with a nod. "Betty will be with you in a minute."

Within seconds, a waitress walked up to them. "How's my favorite little boy?" she said.

Drew glanced at Mac, who was looking shy, still gently kicking his feet under the counter.

"Who did you bring with you today," Betty continued, still talking to Mac.

He took a deep breath. "Aw, just my mom's friend from the boat dock," Mac said.

"Oh, do you work over at the port?" Betty asked Drew, not quite understanding.

"No ma'am, we met at the park. On a dock. I'm Drew."

"He used to be a pirate," Mac said.

"A *pirate*," Betty said in an amazed tone. "What kind of pirate?" She looked intrigued and gave Drew a more thorough inspection for Mac's enjoyment.

"A nice one," Mac said reassuringly.

"Oh, okay, thank the Lord," Betty said, sounding relieved. "What can I get the nice pirate and his first mate to eat or drink?"

"Two milkshakes, please," Drew said.

"Two milkshakes, coming up. I know Mac King wants chocolate, but what about you, Mister Drew the pirate from the boat dock?"

"Chocolate for me also, please," Drew said.

After Betty walked away, Drew raised his eyebrows several times comically saying he couldn't wait for the milkshake. This caused Mac to laugh and kick under the counter again.

"Should we get some food for dinner and take it home to your mama? It's almost dinnertime. What's your mom's favorite thing from here? We could order it and take it home."

"Well, my mom does love chicken nuggets."

"Is that her favorite or your favorite?" Drew asked.

"She likes them, too."

"What does she like the most?" Drew asked. "If I get you the chicken nuggets and her something else."

"Lucy gets a club sandwich like her mama," Betty said, overhearing them. "If it's cold out, she'll switch to meatloaf and mashed potatoes or soup, but I'd go with the club today."

Drew looked up at Betty, smiling at the fact that she knew Lucy's order. "How about two of those club sandwiches and some chicken nuggets for little man." Drew paused and glanced down at Mac. "Is that right? You wanna go with the chicken nuggets?"

"I'd be shocked if he didn't," Betty said.

Mac nodded, agreeing that he wanted the nuggets.

"Lucy gets a substitution on her sandwich," Betty said. "Do you want Patrick to make yours that way, or do you want the regular club?"

Drew didn't care what the substitution was. "He can just make them both the same, that's fine," Drew said.

Betty smiled and gave him a nod as she went to get started on their orders. She spoke to Patrick for a second through the window and she went to make their milkshakes.

Moments later, she put the shakes in front of them. "I put them in a to-go cup for you in case you needed to take them for the road," she said as she set them down. There was a canister of whipped cream in a refrigerator under the counter, and Betty took it out and began adding whipped cream to the top of Mac's milkshake.

"I know Mac wants whipped cream on his," she said. "But how about Drew?"

"Of course," Drew said. He smiled at Mac, and Mac was excited enough that he started swinging his feet again.

"I love your guts," he said to Drew after Betty walked away. He added a little fake laugh.

Drew smiled. "What'd you say?"

"I said, um, I love your guts, because that's what my mama says," Mac said. He took a sip of his milkshake. "So, I love your guts."

"Oh, okay," Drew said. "I love your guts, too, Mac."

CHAPTER 12

Lucy

I saw Drew and Mac coming up the path from my parent's driveway. They had food and drinks with them. I recognized the packaging, and I knew they had been to Carson's on Bank Street. Drew knocked a couple of times lightly, but Mac opened the door.

"What's all this?" I asked, looking at them from my place in the kitchen.

"It smells good in here," Drew said.

"It smells like cookies," Mac said. He came in strutting. He was holding a paper cup from Carson's, sipping on it, and walking with swagger like it was the best day ever. He came into the kitchen. "Whatcha doin'?" he asked.

Mac was happy and confident like he always was, and I smiled and glanced at Drew who had stopped to take his shoes off at the door.

"Yeah, whatcha doin'?" Drew asked, seeing me look at him.

"I'm baking cookies. What are you guys doing?"

"We got milkshakes," Mac said. "And food, too," he said. But he kept going into his bedroom while Drew came to the kitchen.

I made sure there was a spot clear on the counter for him to set down the bags. "You bought dinner?" I said.

"Betty said you'd want a sandwich."

"How do you know Betty?" I asked, staring up at him with curiosity.

He grinned. "I just met her today. Apparently, Mac knows everybody."

"I wonder what Betty was doing there on a Sunday," I said.

"You even know their schedules?"

"No, well, yeah, I guess. I thought she was just there in the mornings now, on weekdays. She must've been filling in for someone."

"She knew exactly what you wanted, so it shouldn't surprise me that you know when she's working."

"Yeah, I basically grew up in that hardware store. I'm still there all the time. I go to Carson's a couple of times a week to pick up stuff for the guys at the store."

"That's a cool place to grow up," Drew said, thoughtfully. He was nodding slightly and looking at me like he might say something else, but he didn't.

I took plates out of the cabinet and began dishing out the food. "It was a cool place to grow up," I said. "And thank you for getting all this," I added, now that the boxes were open and I could see what was inside. "I'll give you some cash."

"Don't even think about it," he said.

"Whose is whose?" I asked, staring at the sandwiches. He looked into the boxes as well. There were chips and a pickle spear in each box.

"They're the same," Drew said.

I began taking them out of the box and arranging them on our plates.

"I'm trying to get you a publishing deal," he said. My head snapped up and my eyes met his. He smiled at my expression. "I didn't want to say anything because it's not for sure yet, but it's your birthday, and I didn't have a gift for you. So, I wanted to let you know that I'm trying. I'm going to contact some of my dad's friends and see what we can do for you. I'm not promising anything, but I feel pretty good about it, especially because your stuff is so amazing." He paused and smiled at me. "So, I guess your birthday present is that I'm *trying* to get you a publishing deal. I'm not sure how good of a present that is, since it doesn't actually exist yet, but..."

"What? It's amazing." I blinked at him. "Are you being serious? Is that even something you could do? Do you have those sorts of connections?"

"Not specifically," he said. "I talked to my dad about it, though, and he said it would be a friend-of-a-friend type of thing. But he thinks he knows a few people who could help you. Some guy named Jim. We already talked about it last night when I went back to the party." Drew reached out and took a chip off of the plate. He popped it into his mouth and took a second to eat it. "I wasn't going to tell you until we talked to someone, but I feel good enough about it to mention it. And I didn't have anything for your birthday."

"You don't need to get me anything," I said. "It was three weeks ago. They just sang to me because—"

I stopped talking mid-sentence because Drew put his hand on my lower back. I turned a little when I felt him do that. We made eye contact, and the corner of his mouth lifted in a slow grin. He was completely irresistible. His mouth was full and perfectly shaped, and that confident smirk made my heart feel like it was too big for my chest. His hand stayed on my back, unmoving.

I went back to what I was doing. I started moving slower, taking my time, getting the rest of the food from the boxes to their plates. I was so lost in thought that I had no idea what we had been saying before he touched my back. Drew held my hand under the table earlier, but other than that, our physical encounters today had been seemingly accidental and fleeting.

But this. His hand on my back was very intentional. His touch was light. He was barely using any pressure at all. But his hand remained there. He was hardly touching me, and I still felt a warm, tingling sensation in my lower abdomen.

"Who'd you talk to at Aunt Tess's house?" I asked.

"Your uncle," he said. "Tess was off painting."

"Did you stay there a while?" I asked. They had been gone a while and I was wondering how they had spent their time.

"Probably fifteen or twenty minutes," he said. "Long enough for him to bake a batch of those cookies. I brought a few of them over to Marvin's apartment. That's when we saw the diner and decided to go."

"Uncle Billy had you make a delivery to Marvin?"

I was finished arranging the food on plates, and I took a couple of chips off of one of them. I ate a chip and I held the other one out casually for Drew. He leaned in and ate it out of my hand. He looked at me when he did it. I held eye contact with him for as long as I could, but I was shy and I had to look away. His hand was still on my back, and all this touching and gazing had me feeling breathless and shaken.

"Yes, I made a delivery," Drew said. "I liked going over there. It was cool meeting Mr. Jones. He was a nice guy. He and Billy both told me to go train at the gym sometime."

"You should. You'd like it over there," I said. "And Mac knows everybody." I added, smiling and nodding. "He goes to the gym quite a bit. He's the first baby, you know, grandbaby or whatever in the family, so my mom and aunt love keeping him. He's always at the hardware store or over at Uncle Billy's gym."

"He was popular at the diner, too," Drew said.

I regarded him thoughtfully. "Thank you for dinner. And thank you for saying that about a publisher. Don't worry if it doesn't work out. Just the fact that you're talking about it and taking me seriously means a lot."

"Of course I'm taking you seriously. I hope you're taking it seriously," he said. "I hope you know how good your stuff is."

"I do," I said. "I take it very seriously, I mean. And thank you."

"Okay, because we're going to find someone for you to talk to."

"Thank you, Drew. Thank you for even trying. That's an amazing birthday present. I really appreciate it. *Maaaaac!*" I added his name in a louder tone at the end of my statement. Drew took his hand off of my back when I yelled for Mac, and I glanced at him with a little smile. "Here you go," I said as I handed Drew his plate.

We went to the table together, and I prayed for my food and Mac's like I always do. It crossed my mind to skip the prayer or at least not say it out loud. I wasn't ashamed of praying, but I didn't want to make Drew uncomfortable since he had already taken another chip off of his plate while I got Mac settled in his chair. Also, if I was being honest, I didn't want to seem prudish. I already felt boring enough with my toddler routine. But I reasoned with myself and realized that I would regret it if I pretended to be someone I wasn't.

I prayed, and Drew prayed with us. He closed his eyes and bowed his head, looking like the mirror image of Mac. We ate, and then Drew spent another couple of hours at my house. He helped me package the cookies in little baggies with three in each.

Mac had his bath and then fell asleep while we were doing all of this. He hadn't taken a nap, so he was exhausted. We left him sleeping in his room while we walked the few steps to my mom's house to deliver the cookies.

Jenny had been going back and forth between houses, but she was at my mom's when we told her goodnight. Drew was planning on leaving, but he walked me back to my place to tell me goodbye first. He was spending the night in Galveston again, and he would be headed back to Houston tomorrow.

He reached out and took my hand as we got to my door. "I don't want to leave you," he said, sounding desperate. His words caused a warm, rushing, sensation to happen in my body. I ached to hear him say those words and it physically affected me when it happened. But I had to be cool. I had to be nonchalant.

Drew had no idea what he was in for with a toddler. We had a great time together today. We had so much fun that he was not thinking straight. He was not thinking clearly. He wasn't remembering that I had a sleeping firecracker in the next room and that I would wake up and do it all over again tomorrow and the day after that.

I motioned for him to follow me into the house. My cousin was really curious about us, and I wouldn't put it past her to spy. "Let's do it in about a month, don't you think?"

"A month of what?" he asked.

"Just take a month where we go back to our regular lives. Where we don't see each other."

"Why would we do that?" he asked, looking genuinely confused.

I couldn't help but smile at his facial expression, but I made a neutral face as quickly as I could. "Because, Drew, these last two days have been... really... good... you know... so maybe we should..."

"If it's been good, then why would you say we shouldn't see each other? That doesn't make sense."

"The thing is... I don't think that we could spend time together and just act like friends."

"We can't. I don't want to do that. I'm not trying to be friends with you."

I let out a little sigh. "Just hear me out, okay? I think we both kind of figured out we're drawn to each other."

"Yes, Lucy. That's what I just said. I don't want to be your friend."

"Okay," I said reasonably. "I just can't help but feel like you'd re-think things if you took a few weeks or a month and paused the newness of it all. I think that would be long enough for you to think about it."

"So, you're saying I have to go away from you for a period of time just to prove that I want to be here in the first place?"

I stuttered, not knowing how to answer that question. "W-well, it's not like that. It's just that I think it'd be smart to pause and take a deep breath. For Mac's sake, and for yours."

He shook his head, confused. "If you don't like me, that's one thing, but I don't see why we should force ourselves to spend time apart just to prove that we still want to get back together at the end of it."

"When you put it like that it doesn't seem like it makes sense, but it does, I promise."

"What happens if I want to come back in a month?"

"Then, I'll take you to Carson's and buy you a club sandwich." I stared at him, feeling the utmost sincerity when I added, "But please don't feel bad if you figure out you want to be my friend, Drew. I would still be happy to be your friend. We could still hang out and you could come see Mac and everything."

"Stop trying to break up with me," he said. He reached out and pulled me close, and I stared up at him.

"I can't break up with you when we're not together," I said. I was being playful, but I regretted it the second it came out of my mouth.

"We will be in three weeks," he said.

"I thought we said a month."

"You said a month *or* three weeks," he said. "Look, Lu, I'll do your challenge if it makes you feel better. I'll wait a few weeks to prove to you that I'm not going to change my mind. But what do I have to do then? Do I just show up on your doorstep when the time is up?"

I hesitated, opening my mouth and then closing it again before deciding what to say. "Yes, Drew, please, by all means.

If you wait a few weeks, and you still think it's a good idea to try to be more than friends with a woman who has a child, please come back. But also know that I won't be mad at you if you don't."

CHAPTER 13

A month later

$\mathcal{A}$s the weeks passed, I realized I had been stubborn and ruined whatever I had with Drew Klein. I knew it was a risky move when I told him to leave me alone for a certain amount of time, but I had no idea I'd be so mad at myself when he failed the challenge.

I should have just gone with it and gotten to know him when he was ready and willing to get to know me. But no, I had to go and try to put him to some kind of test. And enough time had passed by now that it seemed as though we had failed.

If I had to guess why I did this to myself, I'd say I had some fear about getting close to people after what happened to me with my parents and then with Bradley. I thought about Drew a lot, though, during those weeks and I regretted not taking a chance with him.

I never mentioned him to anyone. My family must've assumed it had been his decision to stop coming around, because no one asked me about him either. My mom would have analyzed me if I would have told her about it. She would have figured out that I pushed him away and she would have encouraged me to either go get him or fight against that urge next time. I didn't really want to talk about it. My family just sort of got the picture that he wasn't coming around, and they didn't know if it was a sore subject for me, so they didn't bring it up.

Mac did ask about Drew several times. I told him Drew lived in Houston, and I said that I thought we would probably see him again sometime. I acted really upbeat and happy about it in front of Mac even though I was mad at myself for pushing him away.

I told myself I had gotten what I wanted. Obviously, Drew thought about it and figured out that his life was better off without us. In all honesty, it would have been a difficult transition for any man to make. In one way, I had accomplished my goal. We realized that Drew wanted other things before I got hurt. But in the end, it hurt anyway, so I guess I was sad that I had given up so easily—mad at myself for that.

Drew did make good on his promise to help me find a publisher. His dad was friends with one of the coaches of the Houston Astros, and he knew a player on the team with an agent who also had a few literary clients.

My parents knew I had a publishing deal in the works, and they knew that the introduction came by way of Drew, but even still, they didn't ask me about him. I thought maybe they assumed he broke my heart. Maybe they weren't that far off.

Either way, I got an agent out of the deal. I had a meeting with him where I brought my work along with some of the illustrations from the artist I had hired. I signed a contract with him on the spot. I had gone to the meeting alone, but the terms of the contract were simple, and I didn't hesitate to sign it.

My agent's name was Jim Lewis, and I was so excited about working with him and seeing where all this would lead. Jim loved the hedgehogs and even mentioned talking to someone at a television network about production of a cartoon series. All of this, the meeting with Jim and the signing of the contract and everything, all of it happened without any word from or about Drew. I had no idea what had happened to him. As far as I knew, he had just gone back to his normal life in Houston.

It was September, and Mac had recently started preschool. He had always stayed home with me or my mom, so it was different having him on a schedule where he got up and went to school every morning. He only went four hours a day, Monday through Thursday. But he loved it, and he seemed so happy and independent when I dropped him off.

So, there was a lot of good in my life. I was busy, and I was technically happy with how things were going. No one besides me knew about the nagging regret I felt about Drew.

I had gotten nervous and excited at around the three-week mark, thinking he would show up on my doorstep like we talked about. Then I got nervous and excited again when it had been a month. I hoped he would come, and he didn't. It had been three days since the official one-month mark, and the more days that passed, the more I figured I would never see him again.

It was a Tuesday afternoon, and Mac and I had just gotten home. I had worked on my series while he was at preschool that morning. I wasn't a scriptwriter, but I hashed out some script ideas for a TV pilot and got my thoughts organized with that so that I had something to show to Jim the next time we met. He would then decide if it was an idea worth pitching to someone else.

It didn't have to be perfect, and I still had a few weeks to put all my ideas together, but I wanted to get going on it as soon as I could. I worked on it until it was time to pick Mac up at noon. We ate lunch with my cousin, Tara, and then we went for a long walk on the beach.

Mac took a twenty-minute nap in the shade of a palm tree before we went to the boxing gym so that he could participate in a fitness class they offered for kids three times a week. It was after school from 3 to 4pm, and Mac loved to go. It was for kids up to twelve years old, so Mac was one of the tiniest ones there, but he loved it and begged me to go most of the time.

We had just gotten home from that.

I checked my mail on the way inside and realized that I had a package. It was a large, padded envelope, and it was all taped-up like it had been opened and resealed. They hadn't even done the nicest job of repackaging it. It was bunched up and had black tape all over it. There was a sticker on the tape that said. "This package has been opened, inspected, and resealed at customs."

I turned it over and glanced at the return address. It had been shipped from Italy, I could see that much. The tape was so haphazardly applied that it was covering the name of whoever sent it. All I could see was the bottom of the address.

The packaging indicated that it was *Express 2-day International Mail*, but the postmark was stamped in red ink, and it clearly showed that the package had been mailed on September sixth.

I had to think about it for a second, but I knew it wasn't even close to the sixth right now. I couldn't remember the exact date, but it seemed like it was the end of the month. I was so caught up in the disheveled nature of the envelope and the fact that it had taken so long to come to me that I forgot to simply open it.

"What is it?" Mac asked, but he had already lost interest and began heading into his bedroom.

"I have no idea," I called at his back.

It was hard and light, and it felt like a box. I turned it over, and regarded my name and address that was written on the front side. My brain instantly went to Drew. I desperately wished the handwriting was his, but I wasn't sure. *He wouldn't be mailing me a box from Italy, anyway.* I wasn't thinking straight.

It was difficult to get through two layers of tape with my bare hands, and I almost gave up and went to get some scissors, but I finally got it open. There was a VHS tape inside. It had a sleeve, but it wasn't marked. It was a blank tape, SONY brand, with no indication of what was on it.

I stared at it, feeling a bit like I was in an action movie and there would be a ransom video on it. I had a small entertainment center in the living room, and I went to it instantly and put the tape into the VCR. I could tell it was ready to go because all the tape was on the left side of the spool.

I turned on the TV and got it set on the proper channel. Maybe I should've hesitated or been wary, but I was too curious for that. I stuck the tape into the machine and waited anxiously to see what would play.

It was Drew.

The image of him from the waist up came up on the screen within the first few seconds, and I felt a lump form in my throat the instant I saw him. He was smiling broadly and looking more handsome than ever.

I had no idea where he was, but his surroundings were gorgeous. He was standing outside, and there was an old-world looking cityscape behind him. It wasn't like any place I'd ever been to. I figured he was in Italy, like the package suggested.

He was smiling, and the first sound I heard was him clearing his throat.

I stared at the screen, transfixed.

He smiled and waved.

"Hi Lucy. It's me, Drew." He looked at the camera sincerely. I felt like he was looking straight at me. "Hey, I wanted to let you know that I'm doing what you said. I had a friend from law school, Dylan, who is spending a year in Naples to celebrate finishing law school. He has family here, and as you can see, it's wonderful, and they have a beautiful home." Drew turned and glanced behind him as he spoke, but then he looked at the camera again. "Lucy, listen, I'm all the way over here on the other side of the world. I'm trying to do what you said. I thought about it, and I realized maybe you were right. Maybe I just needed to forget about you and Mac for a while. Dylan had invited me on this trip months ago, and I wasn't planning on coming. But here I am. I called him and made plans, and so far, I've been here a week. And let me just tell you it's wonderful. I'm happy you asked me to—"

I reached out and pressed the *stop* button on the VCR when Mac yelled my name for the second time. My heart was pounding and in the middle of breaking, but I just smiled and did my best to remain patient.

"Yeah, baby?"

"I need to potty."

"Okay, go ahead," I yelled.

Mac was potty-trained and could handle himself in the restroom, but he liked to announce that it was going to happen. I could hardly wait to reach out and hit the play button.

"…try to move on. I go out every night with Dylan. He knows some locals, and they take us different places. Naples is amazing, and we're able to hang out with some really cool people." Drew sighed and adjusted, staring into the camera like he was really trying to look at me. "But here's the deal, Lucy…" He got up close to the camera and whispered. "I still want you. I'm still over here, on the other side of the world, thinking about you. No matter how far I get away from you physically, or how much I try to distract myself, I just can't stop thinking about you. I just keep thinking, *why am I trying to get over this girl*? Why should I get over you, Lucy? That's ridiculous. I don't want to. So, listen. Please listen. I know it's only been like a… week-and-a-half or so, but I'm telling you, I tried to make myself do it, and I'm just not going to change my mind. Being over here without you only makes me realize one thing, and that's that I wish you were here with me. So, here's the deal, Lu, now it's your turn. Now you need to get out on a limb for me. I'm going to New York, and I want you to meet me there. I made reservations. I'll leave here at the end of next week and head back to the States. I'll arrive in New York on the seventeenth. The eighteenth is a Sunday. Meet me at the top of the Empire State Building on Sunday the eighteenth at 6pm. We'll stay at the Four Seasons. We'll spend a week in New York."

He paused, staring at the screen as if he was giving me time to let all of this sink in. I was thankful. I needed time to let it sink in. Both my heart and my mind were racing. I felt a wave of nauseating anxiety when it hit me that he was talking about the eighteenth of September, which had already passed.

"Moooooommm!" Mac yelled, startling me.

I reached out and stopped the tape again, blood pumping.

"Yeah?" I said, trying to be calm.

"I'm finished!"

"Okay, good job!" I yelled.

I waited a second or two for him to say something else, and when he didn't, I reached out and press the play button again. I felt cold sweats as I watched Drew continue.

"I know it's a lot to ask. I know I'm asking you to trust me with a lot right now. I know you'll have to make plans for Mac and flight arrangements." He smiled. "But I know you can do it. I know you can find a way to get to me if you want to. So, there it is, Lucy. Please come. Please come to New York. Meet me Sunday the eighteenth at six o'clock, and spend a few days with me over there. We talked about New York. Remember that? I know you want to see the Statue of Liberty and all of the museums. Just stop this tape, and start making plans to get over here." He put his hands out, palms up, smiling. "I'm not changing my mind about you, so if you want me, just come to New York and get me. I'll see you in a couple of weeks, okay? I love your guts, Lucy."

And just like that, the screen flashed black for a few seconds and then went to static.

I quickly stopped the tape.

CHAPTER 14

sat there for several seconds before tears sprang into my eyes. I didn't mean to start crying, but in this case, I couldn't help it. I felt so many emotions. They hit me like a ton of bricks. First of all, *I love your guts* was something Mac and I said only to each other.

Mac heard someone say *I hate your guts*, and he made it up. But we only said it to each other, and I wondered if Drew knew it from Mac or if it was just coincidence. I couldn't imagine that he knew it from Mac. I also couldn't imagine that it was a coincidence.

It didn't matter. Honestly, I was relieved that Drew had gotten in touch with me at all.

My thoughts were all over the place. I had to figure out the date today.

I went to a calendar that was hanging in the kitchen, and sure enough, today was Tuesday, September twentieth. I went to the living room and watched the tape again just to make sure that Drew was talking about the same September eighteenth that had already happened two days ago. He was.

I cried the whole time I watched it. I wasn't trying to be a baby about it. I just couldn't get the tears to stop flowing. I was relieved and desperately in love at the sight of him, and I loved the fact that he wanted to see me. And then I felt extremely angry when I realized how long it had taken for the package to get to me. My anger turned to hopelessness and fear as I imagined Drew waiting there, at top of the Empire State Building, only to have me never arrive.

I wondered how long he waited there.

I was nauseous at the thought.

All of this was going through my mind as I watched the video a third time.

I sat there after it played through.

I had no idea where to begin.

I was ready to leave on the quickest flight to New York. Part of me wanted to get into the car and drive to the airport. I could work it out with my parents and do that, no problem. *But would Drew still be there? He had said we could stay a week in New York. Surely, he was still there, right?*

I went to the kitchen and picked up the phone, dialing 4-1-1 for information. I had been shedding tears, but it wasn't the type of crying that made me sob. I was easily able to calm myself down enough to place a phone call.

"Operator," she said when she picked up.

"Hey, I'd like to see if I can get a number for somewhere in New York. It's called the Four Seasons. It's a hotel."

"In New York City?" she asked.

"Yes, ma'am. Do I need to call someone else or can you help me with that?"

"I can help you," she said. "Just give me a minute."

"Sure. Thank you," I said. I waited during a few seconds of silence.

"Are you talking about the Four Seasons on East Fifty-Seventh Street?" she asked.

"Uh, I… I actually have no idea about the address," I said. "Is that the only Four Seasons Hotel in New York City?" I asked.

"It looks like it, from what I can see," she said. "Would you like me to connect you? Standard long-distance calling charges would apply."

"How much are those?" I asked, even though it didn't matter.

"You'd have to ask your long-distance provider. I can give you the number if you'd rather place the call another time."

"No, that's okay, connect me, please."

"One moment."

The man who picked up the phone spoke with a British accent. He stated that it was the Four Seasons and asked me how he could help me.

I realized promptly that I didn't have a plan.

"Hello, I'm supposed to be meeting someone there. Well, I was supposed to be meeting them the other day, but there was a mix-up at customs with my package, and it got delayed so I didn't get to..." I trailed off, pausing to take a deep breath. "Basically, I was wondering if my friend was still staying there at your hotel or not. He was there a few days ago, for sure, and I think he had the reservation for a week. Do you happen to have a gentleman staying there by the name of Drew Klein? Traveling from Texas. Well, Italy, but... never mind. He would've checked into your hotel on Sunday the eighteenth, I believe."

"Yes, ma'am, Mister Klein is still with us, would you like me to ring his room?"

"Uh, y-yes sir, please."

"Of course, one moment."

The line began ringing.

I sat there, on pins and needles.

It rang five or six times before clicked over and the front desk guy picked up again.

I told him I had been on hold for Drew Klein, and he asked if he could take a message.

"Do you know when he's leaving?" I asked. "He told me he was booked through the end of this week, but I just wanted to make sure he hasn't changed plans."

"Yes, ma'am, it looks like he still has the room booked through the twenty-fourth. As of now, that's what I'm showing."

"Are there maybe two rooms—one for Lucy King?"

"That one's been cancelled, but I can reserve another room if you've changed your mind and would like to stay at our hotel."

"Thank you, I'll think about it," I said.

I hung up with him, and for the rest of the night, I did nothing but search for the fastest way to get to New York City.

Obviously, I had to get my parents on board because I needed their help with Mac. That was a harder task than I ever dreamed it would be. Even after showing them the video, my parents were hard to convince that I would be okay traveling all the way to New York for somebody who did not know I was coming.

Ultimately, though, I was a grown woman. I reasoned with them about my regrets and my desire to go, and they agreed to help me with Mac. I made spur-of-the-moment flight and hotel reservations. I tried to make a reservation at the Four Seasons, but it was too expensive, so I settled for a nearby hotel that the attendant at the Four Seasons recommended as a cheaper alternative.

So, there I was. One day, I was in Galveston assuming I'd never see Drew again, and the next, I was on a flight to New York City to track him down.

***

My flight arrived that following evening.

It was dark when I flew into the city, and I gawked at the lights at night. It seemed so vast that I had the sensation of being smaller than I thought I was. Everything below me looked like a speck, which made me feel like a bit of a speck myself.

I caught a cab at the airport and gave them the address to my hotel. I planned on going there to get cleaned up first. I had a long night last night, followed by a long day of traveling today.

Drew still had no idea I was coming. I had tried to call his hotel room again this morning before leaving Texas, but he was out. I thought about leaving him a message, but I didn't. It wasn't so much that I wanted to surprise him, it was more that I was nervous. I thought maybe he was hurt by me not showing up a few days ago. I figured I had the best chance of getting him to forgive me if I could tell him what happened in person.

It was just after 9pm when I made it to my hotel. I asked the attendant about the Four Seasons, and he said it was only a few blocks up the street. I had considered waiting until tomorrow to find Drew, but I just couldn't. I put my things in my room, took a shower, and got dressed again in record time.

I called the front desk and asked them to have a cab waiting for me. I had never been to New York City, and it was surreal arriving at night and doing things like taking cabs from hotel to hotel. I felt like I was in a movie. I wasn't sure if you should tip a cab driver, but he had been nice and I was all pumped up with excitement, so I gave him a few extra dollars.

The temperature was cool out, and I breathed in the crisp air when I stepped out of the taxi. The Four Seasons was much grander than my hotel. I walked into the lobby, thinking it was obvious why there was such a price difference.

I felt somewhat small in this city, but at least I was confident in what I was wearing. I had on an outfit I had bought for my first meeting with Jim. It was loose-fitting pants, rolled like high-waters with leather loafers. I had on several layers as a top, including a cotton striped black and white t-shirt, layered with two solid colored linen shirts. It was quirky, but dressy-looking at the same time. Also, my parents had approved, so I knew I looked like a lady.

I was comfortable in my clothes, and it was cool out, but that didn't stop me from almost breaking a sweat as I walked through the lobby toward the front desk. I had thought about different things I could possibly say to Drew, and still, I didn't know quite what would come out of my mouth when I spoke.

"Good evening, I'm Alex, how may I help you?" he said in a British accent.

It seemed that the tall, thin man behind the counter was the same guy I spoke to yesterday. I got so distracted by putting a face with a voice that I blinked and stared at him for a second before I continued.

"Oh, hey, yeah. I actually called last night. I don't know if you remember, but I was asking about someone who's staying here named Drew Klein."

"Oh, yes ma'am. Are you here to see him this evening? I could ring his room if you like."

I wasn't sure that he remembered me from the phone call, but he was trying to be helpful.

"Yes, actually. That'd be great."

He smiled. "Who can I tell him is here?"

"Llll-olli-pop," I said, reluctantly.

"Lollipop?" he asked with a curious, serious expression.

I nodded. I smiled inwardly at the sound of the word *lollipop* being repeated in his British accent, and I had to hold back a laugh at myself for saying that was my name in the first place.

He hesitated as if giving me time to change my mind or tell him I was only kidding.

"I'll ring his room. One moment," he said finally.

"Lady," I added uncertainly, cutting in before he could pick up the telephone receiver.

"Ma'am?" he asked, still wearing a serious expression.

"Lady Lollipop, please," I said.

"You want me to tell Mister Klein that Lady Lollipop is here?" he asked, clarifying.

We were standing in a five-star hotel, and I was pretty sure Alex thought this was one big joke. But he skillfully walked the line between being accommodating and being professional. He gave me a half-smile. "I'll ring Mister Klein and tell him Lady… Lollipop is here," he said, moving slowly and giving me one last chance to back out.

I saw his chest rise and fall as he waited for Drew to pick up. Seeing him breathe reminded me to do the same. I took a deep, calming breath.

CHAPTER 15

---∞∞∞---

"Yes, hello, is this Mister Klein?"

There was a pause.

"This is Alex, here at the Four Seasons front desk. I have a young lady here who would like to speak to you. A Lady... Lollipop."

He stared blankly at the counter while he waited for Drew to speak. Then I saw him glance up at me.

"Yes sir, she's right here."

Alex blinked at me.

"Yes, sir, the young lady indeed has brown eyes."

Sometimes you could hear people's voices coming over the phone, but I could not hear anything Drew was saying at all. There was soft instrumental music playing in the lobby, and the phone's volume must have been low. I was straining to hear but I couldn't.

"Is your name Lucy King?" Alex asked, looking at me.

"Yes," I answered, saying it loud enough that I hoped Drew could hear.

Alex's face changed. He had been stoic before, but he widened his eyes and made a face when Drew hung up on him. He hung the phone up stiffly, staring at me like he didn't know quite what to say. I could tell Alex had no idea whether Drew had hung up out of excitement or out of anger. Honestly, I wasn't exactly sure of myself. My heart told me it was out of excitement, though so I went with it, acting confident.

"I'm going to sit down there on one of those couches to see if he comes down," I said. "Thanks for calling him."

I gave Alex a wave and walked off, heading down the steps and toward one of the couches in the sprawling entryway. Had I not been so nervous, I would have gone to the elevator to stand there, expecting him to come down. But as it stood, it felt like all I could do to sit on the couch.

It wasn't packed in there by any means, but there were a few people spread out in the lobby area, and that was more than I expected for this late on a weeknight.

Minutes felt like hours.

I could hear my heart beating in my ears.

I thought of random things like shoes and pencils to try to calm myself down. I even tried to think of a song to sing in my mind. But any thought besides the ones about Drew seemed forced.

I kept imagining where he was at that very second and wondering if he was on his way down to me. I was sitting up straight on the edge of the couch, waiting, watching, trying and failing to distract myself.

And then I saw him come around the corner.

He was wearing jeans and a t-shirt, and I watched as his athletic-looking body crossed the lobby. He glanced around, searching the sprawling rooms intensely. He said something to Alex at the counter, and I held my breath as Alex pointed my way.

I was already standing when Drew turned and saw me. Our eyes locked, and he instantly came toward me. I walked toward him, and we closed the gap in a short amount of time. We were staring at each other as we came closer. Our expressions were searching, urgent.

He held out his arms, and I walked into them. He embraced me, wrapping his arms tightly around me, holding me. I was completely enveloped. I tucked my head and rested my cheek against his chest, holding him back.

"What are you doing?" he asked. His deep voice filled my ears and his chest moved as he tried to catch his breath.

"I just got the video yesterday," I said, feeling like I couldn't get the words out fast enough.

Drew pulled back, staring at my face, focusing on me. "What?"

"Your video tape," I said. "It got held up in the mail. I just got it yesterday." My words were coming out urgent-sounding because I was urgent. I was desperate. I needed him to know I would have been there. "I would have come here on the day you said. I would have met you anywhere. If I would have known in time, I would have been there."

He pulled back, looking down at me. I was so caught up in the moment that it took me a second to realize he was still catching his breath.

"Are you okay?" I asked.

"Yes," he said. "The elevator was taking forever, so I took the stairs. Twenty-six flights, but don't worry about it."

He was being nonchalant and joking with me, and I smiled as I reached up to touch the side of his face. His cheek was warm and big, and touching it made me feel like I might melt. I was nervous doing it, and I barely touched him, but I could tell how badly he wanted to see me. I could see it in his eyes.

"I would have been here," I whispered, staring back at him.

"You would've?" he asked, his gaze piercing through me.

I nodded and smiled, and then I decided to move. I took his hand and pulled him over to a couch. The lobby was gigantic with seating areas and rooms that led to other hallways. I scanned our surroundings, knowing we had options, but I liked where I had been sitting, so I picked a spot on the same couch.

"Where are you taking me?" he asked.

"To the couch to hang out," I said.

I was wound up from surprising Drew, but mostly I was just happy to see him and so relieved that he wanted to see me.

"I feel like I'm dreaming right now," he said holding my hand tightly.

"I feel like I'm dreaming too. Of course, that might be the malnourishment talking."

"You're hungry? What can I get for you?" he asked, stopping in his tracks. "Really, let me call you in some food. Do you want pizza? Chinese?"

"Chinese," I said.

"Noodles or rice?"

"Noodles," I said.

"Okay, I'll be right back," he said. He gripped my forearms. "Don't go anywhere."

I smiled.

"Don't."

My smile broadened. "Don't worry, I won't."

I watched as Drew went to the desk and talked to Alex, and before I knew it, he was on his way across the lobby to meet me again. I didn't stand up. I just waited for him to come sit next to me. He sat in the corner of the couch, and I turned to face him, kicking my leg onto the couch and getting comfortable.

He looked at me for a second before he reached out. "Come here," he said.

I leaned in, going to him, curling up next to him.

We stayed like that, talking about my trip for the next thirty minutes until our food arrived. Then we sat on that same couch and ate Chinese noodles straight out of the box with wooden chopsticks. Thankfully, using chopsticks was a strong suit of mine. I had my father to thank for that.

My dad had learned to use chopsticks when he spent some time overseas in the war. He had fun using them, and he always took a few extra packs of the disposable ones they gave out at Chinese restaurants so he could teach us how.

I had gotten good at them to impress my father. I was daddy's girl since the day they told me Phillip and I were being adopted. I had always sought his approval, and getting great at using chopsticks had been a byproduct of wanting to impress him.

I used to keep the disposable chopsticks until after dinner, wash them off, and then use them in my room on objects like ponytail holders and paperclips. We had this container of plastic and wooden beads for stringing on necklaces, and I would practice on those, so I had gotten used to managing small, slippery objects. Noodles were easy for me, and I loved that Drew was impressed.

He had ordered two boxes of the same thing, but we ate out of the same box. He was probably meaning to hand me the box when he opened the first one, but instead of taking it from him, I just reached in with my chopsticks and got a bite like I expected us to share.

"You can get it for me," he said, after taking a bite or two on his own. He held the box toward me.

"Are you asking me to feed you a bite?"

"Yes," he said. "Please."

"Are you okay with me using my chopsticks? Or do you want me to get it with yours?"

"Yours are fine," he said with an easy smile. "I don't see why we can't share chopsticks. I'm about to start kissing you, anyway."

"You are?" I asked. I stabbed the chopsticks into the box nervously, trying to get a perfect bite together.

I found that I was better at using chopsticks when I wasn't getting a bite of food for Drew. I reached out and held onto the bottom of the box so that I could get better leverage. My fingers touched his when I did, and that just proved the fact that I was done for. One simple touch of the fingertips, and every cell in my body felt alive with anticipation.

Somehow, I gathered a good bite and fed it to Drew. I was accustomed to feeding my son food, but this was so very different. I was looking at his mouth when I put it in there. I had been thinking about him for over a month, feeling regret, and now that I was next to him, all the little things made me want to swoon.

"Tell me what happened with that agent," Drew said.

And I did.

I told him all about Jim and us working on a pilot for a cartoon television series.

For the next two hours, we sat there and talked. We asked each other questions and caught up on what we had been doing for the last month.

I told him about Mac starting preschool, and we laughed when I recited some of the things he told me about his teacher and his new friends. Drew told me about his trip to Italy and a few of the things he had done so far in New York. He had friends here as well, which didn't surprise me. He knew a lot of people from his dad and through college.

The lobby was quiet once it got to be late. A couple of employees and a few guests were visible, but they were way off in the distance, doing their own thing.

I dug in my purse and fished out a pack of candy. "Lifesaver?" I asked, holding the pack toward Drew.

"Are you trying to kiss me?" He glanced at the people on the other side of the entryway. "We could head upstairs."

CHAPTER 16

———⦻———

*M*y heart raced when Drew said we could head upstairs.
"Drew?" I asked seriously, vulnerably. We were sitting
close on the couch, and I adjusted, focusing on him, looking
him in the eyes. "Can I talk to you about something?" I felt a
wave of anxiousness and I glanced down and fiddled with the
roll of candy, taking the one off the end and popping it into my
mouth.

"Sure, of course," Drew said. "But you're scaring me by
asking that since all we've been doing is sitting here, talking."

I grinned absentmindedly at his statement as I took a piece
of candy off of the roll and held it up for him. He leaned in and
took it out of my hand with his mouth.

"No, no, it's nothing to be... well, actually I don't know if
you should be worried or not. It depends on how you feel about
what I'm about to say." I sighed. "I don't know how to say it
other than just to go ahead and say that I want to take a second
to have a God talk."

"Okay," Drew said, nodding thoughtfully.

"Well, I love God. You should know He's a part of my life and Mac's. He's amazing and He takes care of me, and I… I really do my best to try to be good. I heard one time that sin is like a sharp knife. You know, if you give a two-year-old a big, huge sharp knife, they'd probably cry when you take it away, because to them, it's beautiful and it's shiny, and they don't understand the danger of it. But we, as adults, we have more wisdom. We see the danger in the knife. That's like sin. God is so much wiser than us. He's not just some rule enforcer who's trying to take our shiny things away. He sees what sin is capable of doing in our lives, and out of love, He warns us about it." I sighed and smiled. "I say that to tell you that the decisions I make about how quickly to move forward physically with you, well, they might seem a little old fashioned. There might be an element of false advertising with the fact that I have Mac. It might seem hypocritical of me to say this, but I don't plan on doing that again before marriage. I just feel like I need to keep myself from it until I decide to get married. That's what I was saying about God. It's not because I feel like I have to follow rules or anything, it's just that I've learned, from experience, that it is a wise choice to do that—to wait, you know?"

He stared at me. "Did you think I was asking you to come upstairs so we could…" He trailed off, knowing I knew what he meant.

"I didn't think... no, no, I just, I wanted to have that conversation since I might seem like a little bit of false advertising with—"

"Please don't say that," Drew said, shaking his head and cutting me off. "Nobody's advertising anything. And I know how you feel on the subject, Lucy. You don't have to clarify."

"How? We've never talked about it."

"Yeah, but I can just tell. I see you, I see how you react to things. I wasn't going to even try to do that."

I took a deep breath. "It's just that I came all this way and I could see where you would think that we would... I didn't want you to be surprised when I said I was going back to my own hotel."

"What hotel?" he asked looking surprised.

"The Birchwood."

"You're staying in a different hotel?" He was obviously perplexed. "You said you took a shower before you called me, and I guess I figured you were in a room, but I never would've dreamed it was in a *different hotel*. Why don't you want to stay here?"

"Because the Birchwood was a lot more affordable," I said laughing a little.

"What? No." Drew hesitated but then opened his mouth to speak again. "Okay, first, just know that I'm not expecting things to happen between us, Lucy. I wasn't implying that when I said we should go upstairs. Do I want things to happen? Yes. I really do. But I understand and agree with everything you were saying about being patient. I already knew we weren't going to…" He paused, trailing off and staring at me before adding, "I would like you to stay here, though, and I would like a proper kiss."

His eyes roamed down to my mouth when he said those words. He was barely touching me, and it caused all sorts of bodily sensations. I thought he might go ahead and do it right there that second. He was looking at me like he was about to, but instead, he spoke again.

"And we seriously can't have you staying in a different hotel. That's not happening. I'd be worried about you. We'll get you a room here. I already had one booked earlier, so I know they're not full. And I'm paying for it. I assumed you knew that. I'm getting your room and flight and whatever else you need or want. I'm the one who asked you to come here."

He was speaking slowly, staring at me like I was the object of his affection. He was into me, and I was into him. There was just no better feeling in the world. Actually, there was something even better. Drew loved Mac. We had already talked about Mac tonight, and I could just tell by the things he would say that Drew loved him. Mac was an incentive for Drew and not a drawback. That was a beautiful thing. It's something wonderful when someone you love loves someone else you love.

Thinking about it made me want to mention something I hadn't mentioned earlier. "Hey Drew?"

"Yeah?"

"You said something in your video—at the very end. You said I love your guts." I tilted my head just slightly. "Did Mac tell you that?"

"Yes," he said, laughing. "Isn't that adorable? It's like I hate your guts, but with love."

I nodded and smiled along with him, but I was so curious. Mac and I only said that phrase in the context of really saying we loved each other.

"How did he say it?" I asked Drew. "Did he tell you it's what he and I say to each other, or did he just say it to you?"

"No. He just said it to me. He said he loved my guts. I had to think about it, but then I realized it was like that other phrase turned around. I thought he made it up on the spot for me getting him a milkshake. I thought it was the cutest thing."

"So, he just told you he loved your guts?" I asked, still in disbelief.

"Yeah."

"When?"

"At Carson's that day."

"What did you say to him?" I asked.

"I told him I loved his guts, too."

I looked away, blinking when my eyes stung like I might cry.

"Why, was that the right thing to say?" Drew asked.

"Yeah, definitely," I said, acting casual even though I was holding back tears. My son had told Drew he loved him in a very special way, and Drew didn't even know it. "I just think it's sweet that he told you that," I added.

"I know, I thought it was really cute." Drew sat up, looking for a clock. "Hey, let's go get your stuff and check you out of that other place," he said, switching gears.

He stood up, getting in front of me before reaching out to help me up. Seeing him from that angle, standing over me, he was breathtaking. He wore a confident smile, expecting me to put my hand in his, which I promptly did.

Drew took me by both hands and pulled me to my feet. I was looking at him the whole time, and he went ahead and used the opportunity to lean in and kiss me. He placed a quick, soft kiss on my mouth. I stretched up and kissed him back, holding back a smile at the amount of reaction that was happening in my body.

"Let's go to the desk and get you a room. Then we can go up to my room so I can change. We'll walk to your hotel to get your things. Is it close enough?"

"Yeah, but I already paid for it tonight. I'm sure they wouldn't be happy about giving me my money back since it's so late. Why don't I just stay there tonight and we can switch our reservation over tomorrow?"

Drew stared at me. The lights from the chandeliers were reflecting in his eyes, causing them to sparkle.

"No," he said with a little smirk.

He said it so softly and nonchalantly that I said, "No, what?"

"No, please?" he answered, looking hopeful. "Please just stay here. We can ask the people about a refund, but I really don't care. I'd rather just pay for two rooms and know where you are. I really don't want you to come all the way to New York and then go sleep in a different building. I just wouldn't feel right about it."

Drew put his arms around me and leaned in close to me as he spoke. He put his mouth right next to my ear.

"Please," he said.

The feel and sound of his warm breath on my ear had me leaning into him.

"You'll rarely hear me mention money, Lucy, but for the sake of talking you into staying, I'll just say that I have enough of it to do this. I can pay for three rooms tonight, and it won't be a problem at all. Please let me do that. I want you here."

His hand rested tenderly in the arch of my lower back, and I nodded as I spoke, already agreeing. "Okay," I said. "I'd love to stay here. Thank you."

Drew pulled me toward the desk where we made a reservation for the next three nights. Tonight, I would stay down the hall from him on the same floor, and then tomorrow, I would move into the room next door to him and stay there for the following two nights.

Once we finished at the desk, we made our way to the elevator. Drew held my hand the whole time we were in the lobby, and he pulled me to him when the elevator doors closed behind us.

We were finally alone. He leaned against the wall, holding me to him and staring down at me with a mischievous expression. The sights and smells were all different in New York City. I was dazed by the newness of it all, and then Drew went and did things like grinning down at me irresistibly and making my head swim.

Drew kissed me in that elevator. He was a gentleman about it, but he kissed me deeply, which was a surreal experience in a semi-public situation. I was overcome with desire, happiness, and relief.

We went into his room for a few minutes so that he could change clothes for the trek to my hotel. And before I knew it, we were in the elevator going down and he was kissing me again. He was sweet, patient, and tender, but he was irresistibly persistent—touching me lightly and kissing me any chance he got.

I just loved him.

I didn't tell him as much, but I knew I loved him. It was the real kind of love—the be-together-forever-love.

We decided to walk to my hotel. It was a nice enough part of the city, and I felt safe with Drew. We encountered more people than I thought we would, seeing as how it was after midnight. We passed a few restaurants and bars that were open, and we walked slowly enough that we could take in the sights and sounds. Drew reached out for me constantly, and I stayed close to him, feeling like there was no place I'd rather be.

It took us a half-hour to get to the other hotel and another half-hour to grab my things and check out.

We ended up taking a cab back to the Four Seasons. It wasn't a long walk, but we were tired and we had my luggage.

"It's tradition," he said when he pulled me close and kissed me in the elevator on the way up to our rooms. I smiled in between kisses for saying that, and he kissed me two or three more times before breaking contact.

I officially loved elevators.

Drew walked me to my room. He helped me in with my luggage, and I thanked him and told him I'd be extremely comfortable there. He kissed me again before he left. My heart felt full to overflowing at the way his mouth constantly found mine. He had kissed me so much during our little adventure to the other hotel, that it took a while for me to replay and remember all of the times it happened.

I went to bed late that night in spite of being exhausted. I was elated. I knew I had done the right thing by going to New York. But it wasn't about New York. It could have been anywhere. The right place was anywhere with Drew.

CHAPTER 17

Drew

Four months later
January

*W*inters were mild in Southeast Texas. There was some cold weather, but it very rarely snowed. Once or twice in Drew's childhood, there had been enough snow to gather into small balls and form into a miniature snowman, but there was never any significantly cold weather like there was up north.

Drew had been on vacations to ski resorts in Colorado and even Canada, so he had been in snow that was several feet deep, but that never happened in Texas—at least not down south where they lived.

Drew was thinking about colder weather as he stood outside, watching the kids on the campus of Mac's school. He had offered to pick Mac up because Lucy was out of town. She was in Los Angeles at a meeting with a cartoon studio.

When Lucy was in town, Drew got to see Mac all the time. But Mac had been spending the night with Lucy's parents, so Drew hadn't been able to see him as much in the last few days. He missed him. The plan was to pick Mac up from school and drop him off at the hardware store with Lucy's dad. Drew thought he might stop somewhere and get a snack or drink on the way.

Mac was in preschool, but he went to the elementary school, so there were older kids around. Drew had been standing there contemplating the weather as he waited for Mac. He was thinking about it because it was a gorgeous fifty-five degrees out. Drew had on a long-sleeve t-shirt and no jacket, and he felt fine. Yet these kids were in heavy winter coats and hats with mittens. A few rare ones were in shorts, but some were all bundled up like they were expecting a blizzard.

Drew saw Mac through a window. He smiled when he realized Mac was dressed the best of all of them. He had on little jeans with a t-shirt and a light hoodie. He was wearing a backpack, too, which made him even cuter. Drew grinned at Mac, feeling proud as he watched the little man approach.

Mac was walking with a young woman. She wasn't his regular teacher, but Drew had seen her before. Drew was standing at the side of the entryway, and he moved closer to the door. He stayed back, hidden from the doorway so that he could surprise Mac when they came outside.

"...Mister Drew," the woman said.

Drew heard the teacher say his name as he was getting ready to come around the corner.

"He's my dad," Mac said, causing Drew to stop in his tracks.

"*Your dad?*" she said. "No. It's supposed to be Mister Drew Klein who's picking you up. Your mom's friend."

"Yep. That's Drew. He's my dad," Mac said.

Drew was taking some time off to study for the bar exam. In the last few months, he rarely even went back home to Houston. He had basically moved into the Galveston house so he could be near Lucy and Mac. They had spent a ton of time together lately, but they never had this conversation.

Mac always called him Mister Drew. He told Drew he loved his guts on a regular basis, but the D-word was never, ever brought up. He had never discussed it with Lucy or heard Mac ask about it.

Drew's heart raced. He didn't want to interrupt them while they were having this conversation, and he immediately started making plans to back up and approach the school from a different angle.

"Well, I went to high school with your mom, and Mister Drew wasn't even around back then, sooo..." The woman's tone was calm and reasonable, but her words were so passive-aggressive that Drew's blood began to boil. His temper didn't go through a slow simmer first, he went straight to irate. He stood there, motionless, waiting to hear what Mac would say, how he would respond to her. "Did your mom tell you Mister Drew was your dad?" she continued when Mac didn't say anything.

"She said if God wants him to be my dad, he will. And God does want him to be it, so he is," Mac said.

"Oh, I see," the woman said. "So, she didn't actually *say* he was your dad. I was wondering because… "

She trailed off. Her tone was full of sarcasm that, thank goodness, Mac could never understand. Drew waited there for a few seconds to hear if Mac would respond. *What was he even supposed to say to that? Poor little man.* Drew wondered what was going through his head.

He was about to step around the corner, but then they would have known that he heard them. He wanted to walk out there right then and stop her from saying anything else, but he decided to be patient and back off so that he could go around.

Children were being loud all around them, and Drew easily stepped behind the bushes and away from the doorway. It only took him a few seconds to find the other end of the sidewalk where he could approach the entrance from a different angle. He waited until they weren't looking and he came around the corner pretending to be surprised when they glanced his way, like he had just caught sight of them.

Drew was angry, but he smiled, acting like it was any other day and he had heard nothing. He held his shoulders back and kept his chin up, walking tall, exuding confidence. He could see the teacher react to him. She straightened her posture and ran her hand through her hair.

She wasn't as pretty as Lucy—not even close. Lucy would blow her out of the water in a beauty pageant. Drew realized that his thoughts were mean, but he was protective, and this woman was on his bad list after the way she talked to Mac.

"Hello," the teacher said when they made eye contact.

Drew walked up to her smiling and with his hand extended like he wanted to shake her hand. "Hello, I'm Drew Klein, Mac's dad. Have we met?"

"Oh, yes, I'm Natalie Harris. I'm Mac's teacher's assistant."

Drew reached down and picked up Mac, resting him comfortably on his forearm and balancing him up high, near his chest. Mac didn't always want to be held. He was a busy boy who was prone to want to walk on his own and break out into a sprint when he deemed necessary, which was a lot. He was kind, but he was independent and curious and not lacking energy.

Right then, in that moment, though, he was still as a rock, clinging to Drew. He made himself easy to hold, light in Drew's arms.

"He had a good day today," the teacher said.

"Okay, great," Drew said.

He wanted to say more about being Mac's dad. But all he could think of at the moment was something like, *"Are you ready to go with Dad?"* and that seemed forced and unnecessary.

He looked at Mac. "You ready?"

Mac nodded, holding still.

"Thanks," Drew said, looking at the teacher. He gave her a casual nod and smile before turning to walk away.

That walk on the way to Drew's truck was one of those rare times when Mac did not ask to get down and walk by himself. Drew had been getting to know Mac for months, and there had only been a few times when he let him hold him for an extended walk like this. All of the other times, it was because it was crowded where they were walking or some other extenuating circumstance like it being late and Mac being exhausted.

It wasn't that big of a deal that a child at his age was allowing himself to be held, but it was a big deal because that child was Mac and he never did this. Drew knew it was a picture of Mac's thankfulness even though Mac didn't say a word about it.

"That lady said you had a good day," Drew said.

"Yes, but Johnathan raced me, and then we both had to get in trouble at recess, but I wasn't the one who even asked to race." Mac paused before adding, "But I still beat him."

"Why would Johnathan even try to race you? You are way too fast for him." Drew shook his head a little, looking completely serious like he just couldn't understand it.

"I don't know," Mac said, letting out a little laugh.

For the last four months, Drew had been making himself take things slowly with Lucy. He had been hooked on her since that night at his dad's birthday. He needed her presence in his life, and there was just no way he was going to let her slip away.

But Drew had been extremely patient.

He had wanted to marry her that first night, he had wanted to marry her when she met him in New York, and he had wanted to marry her about a hundred other times since. He wanted to marry her every day. There was never a day that went by that he didn't want to marry Lucy King.

He had been patient, though, and given himself plenty of space and time to back out. They were spending a lot of time together, but they hadn't even made anything official with family and friends. Drew was living in Galveston and only going home to Houston every once in a while, so his family had only met Lucy and Mac a few times.

Drew had been honest with them and told them about Lucy having a son. They weren't upset about it, but they also thought it was a fling that wouldn't last. They assumed he was just spending time with her while he was staying in Galveston to study for the bar.

Drew knew it wasn't a fling, but he didn't argue with them about it. He had been patient all this time. He had given himself enough time to change his mind. But he just kept being certain that Lucy was the one.

This situation where he was nearly jumping out of his skin to validate Mac with that teacher really put him over the top.

Drew figured he was done being patient.

He drove home with Mac in the backseat, thinking about everything. He was supposed to take Mac to the hardware store to drop him off with Lucy's dad, but instead he pulled into a gas station.

"Whatcha doin'?" Mac asked. He had been pretty quiet, but he spoke up when he saw that Drew was making an unplanned stop.

"I was going to ask if you wanted to go to the beach with me. You could come back to my house for a little while, and we could meet up with Pap and Nana later for dinner. What do you think? If you want to come with me, I'll just call the store and tell them."

Mac didn't answer with words. He just nodded and stiffened out excitedly.

Drew parked by the payphone in the front of the gas station, and within a minute he had called the hardware store and made arrangements with Lucy's dad. Afterward, the boys went inside to get provisions for a walk on the beach. Just the essentials—some chocolate milk, and some chips and candy. Drew also splurged for two cans of shredded beef jerky, which Mac had never seen and would definitely love.

CHAPTER 18

———⚬⚬⚬———

Drew

*I*t was too cold to swim, but that didn't stop the boys from taking off their shoes so they could dip their toes in the water at the shore. They left their snacks by the house and went walking on the beach.

Mac was constantly hunting something—shells, ocean creatures, birds. He was always on the lookout to see what he could find, and usually, he would try to chase or capture whatever it was. Mac never did anything halfway.

Drew watched him, feeling proud. He wanted to be an influence in Mac's life. He wanted Mac to be able to call him 'Dad' without a teacher saying anything about it. He wanted to be Mac's dad. It wasn't just so he could have Lucy. He loved the boy as well.

Mac went up the shore a little way, and he stooped down to look at something, after which he turned around and sprinted back to Drew. "They got a dead jelly fish up there,"

Mac announced, breathing so heavily from the sprinting that he bent over to catch his breath.

"Oh, really? How big?"

"Bout like that," Mac said, gesturing with his hands to indicate a foot or so.

"Gaw," Drew said, looking down the shore for it. "Is it nasty?"

"Yeah, real nasty. It was all puffed-up and full of air and sand."

Drew made a sound of disapproval. "Gross. Well maybe some bird will get it and carry it off." He motioned for Mac to follow him as he turned around. "I was going to tell you it's time to head back this way, anyway."

"You think a seagull will eat a dead jellyfish?" Mac asked, thinking about what Drew said.

"I don't know, to tell you the truth. But I know it won't be there forever. Either the tide will carry it off, or a bird, or maybe even flies."

"Naw!" Mac said, thinking Drew meant flies would carry it off all at one time.

Drew didn't explain. His mind was on other things. They walked next to each other for a few steps before Mac took off to investigate some seaweed and driftwood. He came back to Drew when he noticed it hadn't changed since the first time he saw it.

"Hey, you know how Mom's out of town and you're staying with Nana and Pap?" Drew said.

"Yes sir."

"Well, if me and your mom got married sometime, you know, me and you would be living in the same house and everything. And if she ever went out of town like this, I mean, you could just hang out with me the whole time." Drew never dreamed he could be so nervous talking to a four-year-old. "I mean, I'm not saying you wouldn't stay the night at Pap and Nana's anymore, but you know, we'd be at the same house, me and you, and we'd be a family and everything. We might even have to stay in Houston a little more when I'm working. But I want you and your mom to stay with me. Would you be okay with that?"

"You already told Ms. Harris you were my dad, so I guess you are." Mac shrugged nonchalantly, looking straight ahead as he walked.

Drew grinned, but instantly made his expression serious when Mac glanced back at him.

"We need to talk about it with your mom," Drew said.

"Mom already told me we would live with you if you're my dad."

"So, you and your mom already talked about this?"

"Yes, sir."

"What'd she say?"

"To don't ever ask you if you're gonna be my dad."

"Why'd she say not to ever ask me that?" Drew said.

Mac looked at him and shrugged. He caught sight of a piece of a sand dollar near the edge of the water, and he ran over to it and picked it up.

Drew jogged over to catch up with him. "Tell me what she said," Drew said, even though Mac was more interested in the broken sand dollar than he was in the conversation. Mac smiled and started running when he noticed that Drew was going to run with him.

Mac had to take two strides to Drew's one, so Drew easily kept up with him, even when he was jogging. Mac ran and laughed at how easily Drew outran him. He pushed a little harder, but he just couldn't outrun Drew. Drew noticed when Mac started to lose a little steam, and he ran behind Mac, scooping him up, and causing Mac to giggle uncontrollably.

Drew stopped running, but he held onto Mac, tickling him a little more before setting him down. It was a nice big laughing fit—one that had them both carrying on even after Drew set him down.

Drew sat down in the sand, and Mac came to stand next to him, holding onto his back like a little monkey. "I'm going to ask your mom to marry me, Mac. And me and you are going to be partners after that."

"After what?" Mac asked as he came to the side of Drew and plopped down next to him.

"You know, you and me, I'll be your dad, like you were saying."

"I know," Mac said. "I already told it to Ms. Harris because I knew you were gonna say that."

Drew turned and looked at him. "Don't tell your mom we had this talk, okay, though?"

"Why not?" Mac asked, scowling and wrinkling his eyebrows.

Drew smiled at the fact that Mac didn't want to keep anything from her. "Because I really want to surprise her," Drew said. "I think she would really love that. But it won't be a surprise if you tell her anything."

"Okay," Mac said.

"You can't tell her what I said to Mrs. Harris. You can't tell her any of this. She can't know we had this talk. Just tell her I tickled you and bought you beef jerky and stuff, and don't mention the part about me being your dad or marrying me or anything. If you do, she'll know we had this talk, and she'll know something's up."

"What if God already told her?"

"Well, then that's between her and God. But if you mention it, she'll know for sure."

"She will already know for sure if God told her," Mac said in his precious baby tone. "Cause I already knew when God told me."

"What do you mean God told you, Mac? Are you saying you heard Him talk to you?"

"Naw," Mac said, letting out a little laugh.

"What then? Why do you say that?"

"God just said it right here." Mac patted his own ribs.

"He told you in your heart?" Drew asked.

Mac nodded and gave his sides a few big pats with both hands. "He said it in my heart, and in my stomach."

Drew smiled, loving what a little character Mac was. "I think God told my heart and stomach, too, Mac."

They sat there for a minute, watching the waves roll in.

"Hey," Drew said.

Mac looked his way, staring up at him with those puppy dog eyes.

"I'm seriously going to need your help surprising your mom and keeping all of this a secret, okay? Can you do it? Because if you can't keep a secret, then I'd rather just talk to her. I don't want her to have to pretend to be surprised if she knows. Do you see what I'm saying?"

Mac shook his head. "No. I won't tell her. Are you giving her a surprise birthday party or something?"

"No, but I want to ask her to marry me, remember? Once we get married, that's when we'll live at the same house. But before that happens I'm going to ask her to marry me. That's what I'm surprising her with. If you think you're going to tell her about it or say that we had this conversation at all, I would rather just talk to her about it. But if you can keep the secret, then I'll plan something and it'll be a surprise when I propose."

Mac regarded Drew with a blank expression like he wasn't sure what he was talking about, so Drew explained further.

"Do you know what it is to propose to a lady?"

Mac shook his head.

"Have you ever seen a man give a woman a ring and ask her to marry him?"

Mac shook his head again, not understanding.

"Did you know that when a guy and a lady love each other that they get married?"

Mac nodded. "Well, a lot of times, or sometimes, the guy will make a big deal about asking her to marry him. He'll buy a diamond ring and give it to her in some special way. Its tradition to get down on one knee and everything when you ask her."

Mac laughed at that.

"I'm serious," Drew said, smiling a little. "The guy gets on his knees like this..." Drew popped up, kneeling in the sand, looking up, pretending Lucy was standing above him. He made the motions with his hands like he was holding a ring box. "He presents a ring to her and he says, 'Oh, my darling, Lucy, would you please marry me'?"

Mac rolled laughing. He laughed so hard that he leaned over and literally rolled on the sand.

"What? What?" Drew said, smiling but holding his hands out as if wondering what was wrong with his idea.

"You will not say *my darling*!" Mac said.

"Why not?" Drew said, plopping down beside him. Mac laughed again when Drew reached out and tickled him. "Why not?" he asked again.

"Becauuuuse," Mac said, still laughing. "She's not my *Darling* Lucy, she's just Lucy Ann King."

"Okay, okay, I'll leave out the *darling* part, even though I really want to call her that." Drew ruffled Mac's hair, both of them smiling. "But you have to help me keep it a secret."

CHAPTER 19

Lucy

*M*y trip to California was wonderful.

I missed Drew so much, and I obviously missed Mac and my family, but my California experience was amazing. I had been working, pedal to the metal, and the network was excited about the volume of my catalog and the options for storylines. They already had plans to adapt three stories to scripts and they were working on hiring voice actors and animators. I thought my sights were set high when I imagined myself getting a publishing deal, but an animated series was above and beyond my expectations.

The beautiful thing was that they wanted me for me. I didn't have to pretend to know what to do in the publishing world, or the advertising world, or the animation world. All I had to do was live in my hedgehog world and continue to write Garden City stories.

I didn't see the Hollywood sign or try to look at the homes of movie stars while I was in Los Angeles. I didn't go shopping on Rodeo Drive. I didn't do any of the touristy things that the city has to offer. I did make it over to the beach once, but just for one afternoon.

My trip was focused on work, and that was what made it great. If I had been there to enjoy the landscape and scenery, I would have missed my people too much. But as it stood, with all the business and progress that was taking place, the time passed quickly, and I was back in Texas before I knew it.

I was happy to get home. I was relieved to see Mac and hold him. It had only been a few days, and I felt like he grew.

I got home earlier today, and I had reunited with Mac, but I was still missing Drew.

We had crossed paths with our plans. He was in Houston, helping his sister move, so I wouldn't see him for another day or two. We had seen a whole lot of each other lately, and this was the longest gap in a while. I missed his presence. I missed his laugh. I missed his confidence and his logic. We already had inside jokes, things that made us pinch each other.

I was daydreaming about Drew when Mac came into our cottage. Mac had asked to go to the park for a walk, and Mom asked if she could come.

"Are you ready?" Mac asked. "Nana said come on so she can walk Sport."

"I'm coming," I said. "Give me a second to put on my shoes."

Mac was excited about going on a walk. My mom almost never went with us, so Mac was jumping around and talking fast like he was all pumped up.

It was my Mom's idea to go to Oak Bayou. She had been around Drew quite a bit, and she knew the story of how we first met, but I had never taken her to the place.

Mac sat in the backseat with Sport. He giggled and talked the entire time we drove. He was in the best mood, and it made me smile because I figured he was happy to have me back home.

"*Oh, my dar-ling Luuuucy.*" He sang the words from the backseat, causing me to look back at him.

I thought he was going to sing "*Oh, my darling Clementine,*" but then I realized he said my name and sang the song in a completely different tune.

"What?"

"*My darrrr-liiing Luuuucyyyy!*" he sang, out of tune. He was being hilarious.

"What are you singing about?" I said, scrunching my face and being silly with him in the rearview mirror as I drove.

"He's just excited to have his mama home," Mom said, turning to glance at Mac.

Mac continued singing and jabbering in the backseat. He was excited.

Moments later, we parked on the street near the place that would take us to the dock at Oak Bayou. I turned off the car and reached out to open my door.

"Hold on," Mom said from the passenger's seat, putting her hand on my arm to stop me from getting out. "Mac and I are actually going to keep going from here."

"What? Ma'am?"

She turned to Mac. "Stay in your seat," she said.

He nodded and kicked his legs like he already knew that.

"I'll take your keys and drive your car," Mom said to me. "I told Mac we would go for a walk somewhere else, or I'd take him to Pap's store or something—maybe to the taffy shop."

"Yeah!" Mac said.

My heart started beating faster as I realized what was happening. It had to be Drew. My mom was a stable person. She wasn't the type who would drive me out to a deserted road and leave me there for no reason. It made sense that she was telling me to stay by myself because Drew was here. I was so excited to see him that I didn't even care why we were doing it this way.

"Is Drew here?" I asked, looking for his truck. I hadn't seen it when we pulled up.

"He's supposed to meet you at the dock," Mom said, nodding. "I think he's coming on the boat."

I smiled excitedly at her and we both got out of the car. I ducked and glanced back at Mac before I closed the door. His legs were stiff and his little feet were going ninety-to-nothing in a small motion like he was swimming.

"Did you know Drew was coming here?" I asked him. "Is that why you're all excited?"

He nodded.

"You little rascal," I said, shaking my head and smiling at him like he had pulled one past me. "Bye, my love. Have fun with Nana. I'll see you in a little bit."

"Bye, darling!" Mac said, laughing.

"You are a silly goose," I said, widening my eyes at him, which made him laugh even more. He was too funny. He had never called me darling in his life. I wondered where he got it from. I absentmindedly thought it might be from watching television.

"See you later, darling!" he said, unable to stop himself from saying it one last time before I moved away from the door. He cracked himself up with that. He was delirious with excitement. It must've been surprising me along with the promise of going to the taffy store.

"See you later, darling alligator," I said to him, interjecting his new favorite word and causing him to laugh even more. I stepped away from the car, shaking my head and smiling at my mother. "Why's he calling me darling?" I asked her.

"I have no idea," she said. She urged me along, switching places with me so that she could drive the car. She reached out and hugged me before I could step away.

"I love you, my girl. Have fun, okay?"

"I love you too," I said. I leaned over and said goodbye to Mac before jogging off, searching for the trail that led to the dock.

The dock wasn't visible from the road, but it was only a short distance down a trail. It took me a minute to get to the spot where the trail opened up, and I could see Drew's boat once I got there. It was tied to the dock. I recognized it from a distance, and I jogged that way, feeling like I couldn't get over there fast enough.

I saw Drew when I got closer. He was sitting on the end of the dock, and he stood up when he heard me approaching. Boy, was he a sight for sore eyes. He was barefoot and his jeans were rolled up, and seeing him standing on that dock made me realize how much I missed him.

There was a quilt spread out over the end of the dock with what looked like a basket. The whole scene was inviting, but all I really cared about was the man coming my way, smiling at me. Drew slowly made his way to me, coming closer to where the dock met the land. I was moving quickly and I had some momentum by the time I made it onto the dock.

I didn't hesitate. I flung myself into his arms. He saw me coming, and he braced himself, turning with me in his arms, both of us laughing as we collided.

"I missed youuuu," I said. "I'm so happy you're here. I thought you had to help Brian and Michelle. What happened?"

He let me down on my feet, but he kept a hold of me, smiling at me before leaning down to place a swift but soft kiss on my neck. "Yeah, no, they are moving this week, but they have movers. I wasn't even in Houston."

"You weren't? I asked, shocked.

"No, I just wanted to surprise you."

"You did! This is so cool. It looks like Evelyn's in on this." My mom's friend, Evelyn, had eclectic, expensive taste, and I recognized the quilt and knew it was hers.

"She got all this together for me. That basket's full of food— all sorts of stuff. She did that, too. She made us a picnic."

I didn't even respond. I was relaxed and felt so happy to see him. I leaned into him, gently resting my head on the side of his chest. His chest rose and fell. It was cool out, but his coat was thin and I clearly saw and felt his chest moving as he took a deep breath. He smelled so nice. I stretched up and kissed underneath his jaw. "I missed you."

"I'm so nervous," he said. "I didn't think I would be this nervous." His tone was serious, and for a second, it worried me. I actually wondered if he brought me there to break up with me, and then I remembered that there was a blanket and he was currently holding onto me.

"Why are you nervous?" I asked, pulling back and looking straight at him.

"Because," he said. He gestured around us. "Look what I'm doing here."

"What are you doing?" I asked. I knew I was missing something.

"I'm trying to propose to you," he said.

"You are?" I said, my head quickly shifting around, looking around, taking it all in, feeling genuinely shocked. The thought had not crossed my mind at all.

"I thought you just missed me and made a cool picnic."

"Evelyn took care of the picnic. I was too worried about getting a ring, and shaving, and figuring out what I was going to say to you... which I've already wrecked, obviously."

"What do you mean you already wrecked it? Are you not asking me now?"

"No, no, I am going to ask you. I'm definitely asking you. I just already kind of blew it with telling you what I'm doing here instead of just doing it. I said my plan instead of doing it." He took a deep breath.

I smiled at him. He was genuinely nervous, and it was odd for him because he was always so calm and collected.

"Well, I would've said 'yes' no matter how you asked it."

He grinned at me, staring straight at me.

"This was a great idea for a place to propose, by the way," I said, looking around. "Good plan."

"Yeah? I had other plans, too, all sorts of ideas about pirates and eye patches. I was going to come in on the boat and pretend we were strangers and give you the ring again like that first day. But then I was early getting here, and I wanted to come up here and see what all Evelyn had done. And then, I just felt unnatural to go back out on the boat and wait for you out there."

I stared at him for a minute, taking it all in before I said, "Did you just say there was supposed to be eye patches involved?"

He let out a little laugh and nodded. "Just one eye patch, but yes."

"Your plan included an eye patch?"

He nodded.

"Did you purchase one and bring it with you, or was that just an idea you had?"

"Oh no, I have an eye patch. It's just a little plastic toy one. That's probably why I didn't go through with it."

Drew was relaxed now. I could tell by how he was smiling and talking.

"Where is this eye patch?" I asked.

"In my pocket."

I grinned a little. "Are you joking with me?"

"No. I'm one hundred percent serious."

"Is there a real eye patch in your pocket right now?"

"Yes. Not real. It's a toy. But there is one."

"That's the best thing I've ever heard." I stared at him. "Which pocket? Your jacket pocket, or your jeans?"

"My jacket," he said.

"Can I dig in there and get it?"

"Of course you can."

Drew stayed there, unmoving, with his arms wrapped around me. I smiled at him as I shifted to dig in his pocket. Instead of finding an eye patch, I found a small box. I knew it was a ring box. My eyes met his the instant I figured it out.

"That's not an eye patch," I said.

"You have your hand in the wrong pocket."

I hesitated, blinking once as I stared at him. "You're really doing this," I said as more of a statement than a question.

"Yes."

"Can I look at it?"

"The ring?"

I nodded.

"Yes. It's yours."

"Hang on, let me see this first..." I started digging in his other pocket, searching for the eye patch. His keys were in there, but along with them, I found something flat and plastic that was definitely an eye patch. I smiled at him when I felt it.

"There is one," I said.

"I told you," he replied.

"Would you let me put it on you?" I asked.

"Sure."

I pulled out the black plastic eye patch. It looked like it came with a kid's Halloween costume. I let go of the ring box just long enough to use both hands to put it on him. There was a thin elastic band and I stretched it over his head, gently positioning and securing the eye patch over one eye. I pulled back and stared at Drew once it was straight.

"Not bad, actually," I said.

Drew grinned and nodded. "I know. That's why I was going to wear it. It looks pretty good on me."

I pulled back and stared at him, taking in the moment for what it was. I thought about how I lived in fantasyland all the time, and I took a second to appreciate how wonderful it was that my proposal included my suitor dressing up in an eye patch.

The definition of ideal was obviously different from one person to another, but the sight of Drew dressed up in an eye patch was like magic to me in that moment.

"So, Captain Klein, did you come here to bring me some more stolen treasure?" I asked.

"I do have treasure for you. You've already found it. You've been rifling through my pockets."

"Oh, was that for me?" I asked feigning surprise. I dug in his pocket and took a hold of the box again. "Is this really for me?" I asked, staring up at him before I opened it.

"Yes."

I reached up and flipped the patch where it was resting on his forehead and no longer covering his eye. That way I could stare straight at him. He actually looked handsome wearing that thing around his head. He looked fierce and dangerous, and I smiled, thinking he'd look good in anything.

I held the ring box between us, but I didn't open it. I held it there, deciding if I had the nerve to look inside. I rested my head on his chest. I had missed the light, woodsy smell of his cologne. I wanted to bury my face in his shirt and stay there, breathing it in all evening. I had seriously missed him—I had physically missed his presence near me. My body ached to be next to Drew.

"You can open it," he said.

"I know. I'm just taking a second. I missed you."

I finally pulled back and opened it.

I stared inside.

I was expecting it to be smaller than the other one. I was prepared for that. Drew would know it would be safe to assume I wasn't the type of girl who needed a gigantic wedding ring. It was different than the one I had sold, but it wasn't smaller. This one was vintage-looking and full of charm whereas the other one was modern, clean, and sharp.

This was, no doubt, the perfect ring for me.

I glanced up at Drew. "I love it."

"Good," he said. "See if it fits."

CHAPTER 20

I slid the ring onto my finger and stared at it, feeling humbled and not knowing quite what to say to Drew. I didn't think I wanted a big diamond, but now that it was sitting on my finger, I felt like I never wanted to let it go.

Because of my speechlessness, I almost made a joke about being glad he didn't toss it into the bay, but I kept quiet. I was glad I did because Drew spoke up and what he had to say was much better.

"You were in California, Lu, and I was missing you so much. I was counting the minutes till you got back." He took a deep breath. "Look, I've been trying to go slow with this relationship. Uh, I mean, I guess we're not really going slow, but slower than I wish we were going. Lucy, look, I'm ready to just be with you. I'm ready to start a life with you and Mac. Is it possible that we just jump in to the part where we make our plans with each other from now on? You know, be a family? I talked to Mac, and he's okay with it. So, I figured if you and I are both okay with it, then I can't see any reason why we need to keep waiting."

And then, Drew turned into the Senator's son—the well-mannered gentleman who kept to tradition. He went down on one knee, but he stayed close to me, holding onto me, holding my legs gently, looking up at me. I felt tempted to protest, like I should excuse him from getting on his knee and tell him to stand up, but he didn't give me time for any of that. He just started talking.

"Lucy King, I want to come home to you every day. I want my house to be your house. I want to be Mac's dad, and for us to have more Macs."

I laughed at the thought of that. Tears filled my eyes as I stared down at Drew.

"Please marry me," he said.

"Yes," I said, pulling him to his feet.

I hugged him tightly.

"Soon?" he asked.

"Whenever you want to. I love you, Drew. I feel the same way you were saying. I was over there in California, wishing you were with me. And then I got home and wished you were there waiting for me."

"I am waiting for you," he said.

He squeezed me one time before letting go and pulling me toward the end of the dock. Drew went onto the quilt, stooping to crawl once he reached the edge of it. I watched his lean body stretch as he reached out. Evelyn had left two pillows near the basket, and Drew pulled them onto the quilt with him. He placed one behind his own head, relaxing onto his back and crossing his legs casually. He placed the other pillow next to him and patted it as if waiting for me to lie down. I couldn't wait to.

I took off my shoes before stepping onto the quilt. I stooped to my knees and crawled onto the quilt with Drew. Instead of lying beside him, I sat cross-legged with my legs touching his side so that I could stare down at him.

I leaned down and kissed the top of his forehead, and he lifted his chin and stretched upward, bringing his mouth closer to mine. I kissed him again, this time on the mouth, and the sheer desire that rushed through my body caused me to lean in and kiss him a little deeper, to open my mouth a little.

He wrapped his big hands around my arms, pulling me in. I propped my weight onto my hand and rested it on the other side of his shoulder so that I could get better leverage over him. He put his hand on my side, and the combination of that and the taste and feel of his lips... well, for goodness sake.

I leaned even closer, getting to a new position where my legs were out to the side rather than crossed. I broke contact with him while I readjusted, but I came right back to him, and I was able to get comfortably closer this time.

He wrapped his arms around me, and we went straight to kissing again. We had missed each other, and our mouths just kept touching over and over. I smiled at him between some of the kisses. A barge passed in the distance. We could hear that and the gentle lapping sound of the water as it hit the dock, but otherwise, it was quiet and we were alone.

For the next who-knows-how-long, we barely talked. There was a span of at least a half-hour where we just stayed there on the dock, kissing gently, tenderly, saying nothing. It never got old. I would start to pull back or say something, and then I'd just kiss him again like I couldn't help myself.

He loved it. I could tell by the way he smiled and the way he gripped onto me at certain times during those moments.

We stayed on the dock for the next couple of hours, eating the lovely meal Evelyn had packed. There was bread and cheeses with meat and nuts and fruit. It was delicious, and Drew and I ate while we talked.

Drew wasn't a man to beat around the bush. He asked direct questions, and we talked about what our life might look like after he took the bar and started practicing law. He would need to be in Houston, at least at first. His father's firm was there, and Drew was all set up to practice at it. He would need to get a few years under his belt before he tried to become a judge. We talked about trying to settle in Galveston rather than Houston in the long term, and Drew said he could see us doing that. But really, I didn't care. I would have followed him way farther than Houston.

We took the boat back to the marina before he gave me a ride back to my house. Mac was at my parents' place, so we stopped by there to get him. My brothers were home, and everyone was down in the living room with a basketball game on the television.

My mom headed to the door as soon as we came in. Mac was close on her heels. My brothers stayed where they were, and my dad got up and started coming our way. "Let me see," Mom said, staring straight at my hand.

"See what?" I asked, confused, pretending I had no idea.

Mom glanced at me and then Drew with a wide-eyed expression.

"I'm playing with you," I said quickly.

I stuck out my hand, and my mother grabbed it, staring at my ring. "Oh, my goodness, it's so beautiful on you, Lucy. I just love it, baby, congratulations!"

The guys in my family got curious at that point and all headed over toward us.

"Did you say *oh my darling*?" Mac asked.

The idea of calling me darling was hilarious to Mac for some reason because he cracked up as he said it again.

"I might have, actually," Drew said, seriously answering Mac's question.

"I think he might have," I said nodding and staring like I was trying to remember. "It was all very official. I think he did call me his darling."

This caused Mac to jump up-and-down, stiff-legged from pure excitement. It seemed like he thought the word darling meant we were already married.

We stayed at my parents' house for a while, catching them up. We told my family about the spread Evelyn had set out for us. My mom had been out there and helped her, but it was news to my dad and brothers, and they were curious about it.

I hadn't seen most of them since I got back from California, and I told them about the pilot animation and about my trip in general. It was Drew's second time to hear it all, so once we started talking about that, he went off with Mac to see the line of diecast cars that extended the entire length of the living room. He could hear us from the other room, and he chimed in a few times.

"They told her they were going to try to have it ready for the fall premiers," Drew said.

"This fall?" Evan said.

My littlest brother, Evan, was the only birth son of our parents. Phillip and I had both been adopted. They loved us as if we were their own children, and there was never any feeling that they loved Evan more than they loved us. I honestly didn't even think twice about it, but Phillip had always been really competitive with Evan. I wondered if it was a guy thing or if Phillip felt like he had something to prove. They were close, but Phillip had a bit of a chip on his shoulder. It wasn't a surprise when Evan asked if my show would be ready 'this fall' and Phillip popped him upside the back of the head and sarcastically said, "No, in three years from now... of course this fall."

"It was a good question," my mom said.

"This fall," I said, nodding at Evan. "If all goes well, it will premier in September, when the new shows come out."

"What's it going to be called," Evan asked, unaffected by Phillip.

"Garden City," I said. "I saw a storyboard, and it looks really good. Not exactly the same as the woman who illustrated the books, but still really good. The hedgehogs are chubbier in the cartoon. They're so cute."

Mac came up to me and I reached down to pick him up. "We need to be going," I said.

"Aw, congratulations," Mom said, hugging my neck. "We're so happy for you two."

We spent the next couple of minutes saying goodbye to my family, and afterward, Drew walked Mac and me back to our cottage. It had been a long, exciting day for Mac. He hadn't had a nap, and he was pooped and ready to go to sleep. It only took me ten minutes to bathe him and get him ready for bed.

Drew was still out in the living room when we finished, and Mac went out there to tell him goodnight. Drew was sitting on the couch, and Mac ran over to him, jumping into his lap. Drew held onto him, and they had a conversation. They spoke quietly enough that I could not hear what they were saying.

I was curious, but I wanted them to have privacy, so I didn't go over there. I just stood there and waited for Mac to come back so I could tuck him in. They smiled as they talked, and my heart felt full.

Mac ran over to me after a minute, and I tucked him in. I prayed for him, but we skipped the story tonight. He asked for a story every night, and I told him one most of the time, but Mac was sensitive and he knew when I had other things on my mind. He knew it was a special night for Drew and me, and he didn't even ask me to tell him one.

"I love your guts," I said, kissing his forehead.

"I love your guts, too. And Dad's guts."

My heart broke a little when he said it. It was almost like hearing Mac say that word made him seem vulnerable. I was instantly afraid he would be let down. And I almost told him not to say 'Dad' yet. But then I realized there was no reason for me to do that. Drew was going to be a great dad. He wasn't going to let Mac down.

I smiled at my precious boy. "Dad loves your guts too," I said, turning off his light. "Night, see you in the morning," I added.

"Night, see you in the morning," he said sleepily.

Drew was watching a movie when I came into the living room. I sat on the couch with him and we finished it together. Both of us were hard workers. He studied diligently for his exam and I worked continually either as a mom, at the hardware store, or writing stories. But every now and then, we would just sit and stare at the television, and this was one of those times. I'd seen the movie before and I didn't care. I really didn't watch it. I thought about the proposal at the dock and all that was said between us tonight.

Things felt different.

There were those rare times in life when something happened during the course of your day, and you just felt different afterward—like getting saved, or finding out you were pregnant. They were rare, but this was one of those days where I was going to bed markedly different than I woke up.

I sat there, absentmindedly staring at the Michael J. Fox movie that was playing on TV, thinking of everything and pondering our future.

"I better head out," Drew said, once the credits started. "I know you have to get up early to get Mac to school."

"Okay," I said. I knew he was going to kiss me goodbye, and I couldn't wait. My body felt alive with sensation because I knew it was coming.

I sprang off of the couch and went to the kitchen where I had a small dish full of candy that I used for occasional bribery. I ate a peppermint. I put it into my mouth and chewed it up. I was still working on it when Drew came into the kitchen, smiling at me mischievously.

"Why are you coming in here eating mints?"

"Because," I said smiling and acting shy. "I wanted one."

"Nu-uh, I have you figured out. You always eat candy when you want to be kissed."

He came up to me, and I went smoothly into his arms, leaning into him gently, being purposefully soft and warm as I got close to him. He held me back, being equally gentle.

He loved me. I could feel it. He wasn't just with me to help me out. He didn't feel bad about me being a single mom. He simply loved me. He wanted to be next to me. He loved me so much I could feel it coming off of him.

EPILOGUE

⸺∞⸺

Three years later

*T*he attempt at a Garden City cartoon series was an utter disaster. I had a difficult time working with the studio, and they ended up canceling production before the first three episodes were complete. I got freaked out that they would try to take my work and rebrand it to make something similar, but Drew was with me every step of the way and he assured me that things like this happened all the time and we would just move on.

At the time, it didn't seem that easy. Right then, it felt terrible. I knew God well enough to know that He would use some of our hardest moments for our good, but when it all went down, it was an unexpected, unwelcome blow. One that came at a time when I had a lot of other changes in life.

The other changes were good, I just had a lot going on. Drew and I got married that spring, and we moved to Houston so that he could start his law practice there. It took a little adjusting for me to live near his parents instead of mine. The Kleins were cordial to me all along, but it took time for them to get used to the idea that their son was married and they were suddenly grandparents.

They had warmed up to me as years passed, but that was another thing I was wrestling with right at first. As funny as it sounds, looking back, I could appreciate that cartoon deal going south was actually a good distraction from the awkwardness I felt with Drew's parents during those early months.

I still worked with Jim even after everything that had gone down with the production deal out west (some of which was his fault). We moved forward and made a book deal with a publisher, after which my characters went through another redesign.

This one finally took. We released a ten-book series the following year, and by God's grace, it caught on with early readers. Drew had been more active in the contract process with this one, and I was so thankful to have his legal advice. I didn't comprehend the business or legal side of publishing like Drew did.

We had settled into a routine where he helped me with certain parts of my job in addition to doing his. All this while trying to make parenting our top priority. Drew legally adopted Mac and we changed his surname to Klein to match Drew and me. We gave Mac a say in changing his name, and he wholeheartedly wanted to do it. It was sweet how much he wanted to.

And then, the year after Drew and I got married, we had a baby girl, Katherine (or Katie) Grace. She wasn't even two when her brother, Andrew James IV was born.

I wondered how Mac would take it, having his little brother named after Drew. I had grown up with my brothers' dynamic, and I witnessed Phillip always feeling like he had to compete with Evan.

It seemed to be different in my own little family though, thank goodness. Andrew was still just a baby, but I could sense Mac's tenderness toward him from the start. Mac felt like he had nothing to prove. He loved Andrew and Katie with his whole passionate little heart. He was extremely protective of both of them. In fact, he was being protective at this very moment.

"Mama did you get Andrew and KK a blanket?" He asked the question while I was getting the babies out of the backseat of my car. It was a cool fall evening, and Mac was playing his second season of peewee football. He had his helmet on already, and he was excited to get out on the field, but he came back to ask me that once he realized how cool it was out there.

"Yes, baby, I have plenty of blankets."

"Okay!" he said, turning back around.

Drew's parents met us at the field. They loved watching Mac play football. They had softened to me significantly over the years, and we had a good relationship now. Drew's mom came to me when she saw us pull up, and she took baby Andrew from me so I could hold Katie and my bag.

I greeted her and thanked her for the help, and we took off toward the field. Drew's dad came our way, and once we met up, he took Katie from me. He leaned in and kissed my forehead. "Hey sweetheart."

"Hey," I said.

"I'll take Katie up there with Cindy and the baby." He settled Katie on his arm.

"Okay, I'm coming with y'all, though," I said.

"Well, Drew's here," he said. He nudged his chin toward the parking lot, and I looked over my shoulder to see Drew's truck as he was parking.

I smiled. "Okay, we'll meet you in the stands in a second. And Dad will be with me, too," I added staring at Katie.

She nodded and held onto her grandpa, and I waved at them before I took off, going back toward the parking lot.

Drew was still in his truck when I got back to the parking lot. I couldn't see him until I made it down the line, but I soon realized that he was staying in the driver's seat and not getting out.

Cars were parked so close that he didn't see me until I was basically at his passenger's door. I opened it and peered through the cab, looking at Drew.

"Aren't you coming?"

My husband smiled at me. He was growing a little facial hair, and I loved the way it looked on him.

"Come here," he said, patting the seat next to him. "Come sit in here and sit with me for a minute."

"What's going on? Is everything alright?"

"Yeah, just come here for a minute."

I climbed into the truck. I left my stuff in the passenger's seat and went to sit closer to Drew. He pulled me onto his lap. I was more at home there than anywhere else in the world. I didn't care that we were in the middle of the parking lot. I barely noticed. No one could see us, anyway.

He adjusted so that he could hold on to me, pulling me closer and holding me by the waist. It was cramped, but I didn't care. All I wanted was Drew. He kissed me, and the feel of his soft lips sticking to mine after a long day of not seeing him still left me breathless. I took my time, sitting there and giving him a proper greeting.

"How was your day?" I asked, pulling back just far enough so that our mouths weren't touching.

"Good," he said.

"You?"

"Good."

"Hey," he said.

"What?"

"Do you remember that night when I brought you to my dad's birthday party?"

"Of course I do," I said. "We talked about it the other day."

"Yeah, but do you remember when Blake was going crazy in the little kids' area and you went over there and talked him down?"

"Yes, I do," I said.

I slipped my hand on the inside of his jacket. There was only a thin layer of fabric between my hand and his chest, and I could easily feel the warmth and the hard muscle. Our eyes met and I flexed my hand, slowly touching him, feeling his chest, loving on him.

He took a deep breath. "That night you told me you were going to do something to my nephew. You looked at me and told me you were going to set him up to be a hero. That you would put him in a position where he could step up to a challenge. And you did just that. I watched you do it. And what I'm saying is that you do the same thing to me. You set me up to be a hero. And you would think I would feel like I'm being manipulated since I know what you're doing, but I don't. I like it that you do that. I love it that you expect the best of me."

"I do expect the best of you. But what's making you say all this?"

"Because we're a team. I expect the best of you, too. And you just keep delivering. You're capable of great things, and they just keep happening because of your hard work."

"What's going on?" I asked.

"You got a deal for another animated series."

"You're joking. When? What happened?"

"Jim tried to call the house, but he couldn't get you, so he called my firm just a few minutes ago."

"Yeah, I had the kids over at Brian and Michelle's. What did he say?"

"That a big network executive called him with an offer for you. They want to produce a whole season."

"A network executive from where?"

He shrugged wearing a sly grin. "Aw, nothing. Just a little network called the Disney Channel."

"You're kidding."

"I would not joke about that," he said.

"Is it for sure?"

"Yes. We'll have a lot of details to work out with the contract, but yes, it's for sure. Jim has been talking to them for a while. He just didn't want to say anything and get your hopes up before he knew."

"Is it seriously happening?" I asked.

"Yes."

A wave of excitement and adrenaline hit me, and I held onto the sides of Drew's face, pulling him in for a kiss. He brought his hand to the back of my head, kissing me back.

He had been my husband for long enough that the guess work was out of it. He knew exactly what to do. It was with expert precision and a perfect mix of tenderness and urgency that he kissed me. His mouth was warm and it tasted like heaven.

In that moment, the cartoon deal didn't really matter. It was just Drew and me. I loved him and he loved me, and all was right with the world.

The End
(till book 4)

Other titles available from Brooke St. James:

Another Shot:
(A Modern-Day Ruth and Boaz Story)

When Lightning Strikes

Something of a Storm (All in Good Time #1)
Someone Someday (All in Good Time #2)

Finally My Forever (Meant for Me #1)
Finally My Heart's Desire (Meant for Me #2)
Finally My Happy Ending (Meant for Me #3)

Shot by Cupid's Arrow

Dreams of Us

Meet Me in Myrtle Beach (Hunt Family #1)
Kiss Me in Carolina (Hunt Family #2)
California's Calling (Hunt Family #3)
Back to the Beach (Hunt Family #4)
It's About Time (Hunt Family #5)

Loved Bayou (Martin Family #1)
Dear California (Martin Family #2)
My One Regret (Martin Family #3)
Broken and Beautiful (Martin Family #4)
Back to the Bayou (Martin Family #5)

Almost Christmas

JFK to Dublin (Shower & Shelter Artist Collective #1)
Not Your Average Joe (Shower & Shelter Artist Collective #2)
So Much for Boundaries (Shower & Shelter Artist Collective #3)
Suddenly Starstruck (Shower & Shelter Artist Collective #4)
Love Stung (Shower & Shelter Artist Collective #5)
My American Angel (Shower & Shelter Artist Collective #6)

Summer of '65 (Bishop Family #1)
Jesse's Girl (Bishop Family #2)
Maybe Memphis (Bishop Family #3)
So Happy Together (Bishop Family #4)
My Little Gypsy (Bishop Family #5)
Malibu by Moonlight (Bishop Family #6)
The Harder They Fall (Bishop Family #7)
Come Friday (Bishop Family #8)
Something Lovely (Bishop Family #9)

So This is Love (Miami Stories #1)
All In (Miami Stories #2)
Something Precious (Miami Stories #3)

The Suite Life (The Family Stone #1)
Feels Like Forever (The Family Stone #2)
Treat You Better (The Family Stone #3)
The Sweetheart of Summer Street (The Family Stone #4)
Out of Nowhere (The Family Stone #5)

Delicate Balance (Blair Brothers #1)
Cherished (Blair Brothers #2)
The Whole Story (Blair Brothers #3)
Dream Chaser (Blair Brothers #4)

Kiss & Tell (Novella) (Tanner Family #0)
Mischief & Mayhem (Tanner Family #1
Reckless & Wild (Tanner Family #2)
Heart & Soul (Tanner Family #3)
Me & Mister Everything (Tanner Family #4)
Through & Through (Tanner Family #5)
Lost & Found (Tanner Family #6)
Sparks & Embers (Tanner Family #7)
Young & Wild (Tanner Family #8)

9 781400 333011